KATHRYN RAISED HER EYES TO THE FACE IN THE PAINTING.

The woman had the most arrogantly beautiful countenance she had ever seen. Sensuality pouted in the full lips, pride flared in the exquisite curl of the nostrils, and the eyes— Kathryn felt a shiver of emotion ripple along her flesh as she met the challenge of those strange, light green eyes framed in long black lashes. The eyes caught hers, held them.

Deliberately Kathryn forced herself to look away. It was then she noticed a card tacked to the wall beside the picture frame:

LADY NADINE ELSINGHAM
by Adrian Bart
1774

Suddenly she felt dizzy, felt her mind drift into darkness.

She did not know how long she had been drifting, but she came awake with a start. Then she looked at herself and saw a stranger—a stranger dressed exactly like the woman in the portrait....

The
ELSINGHAM PORTRAIT

Elizabeth Chater

FAWCETT COVENTRY • NEW YORK

For Margaret, my first friend

THE ELSINGHAM PORTRAIT

Published by Fawcett Coventry Books, a unit of CBS Publications, the Consumer Publishing Division of CBS Inc.

ISBN: 0-449-50018-7

Selection of the Doubleday Romance Library

Printed in the United States of America

First Fawcett Coventry printing: February 1980

10 9 8 7 6 5 4 3 2 1

One

Kathryn Hendrix entered the fashionable restaurant at exactly noon. Donald had said "about twelve," but she had a horror of being late for a treat which had been drilled into her during her lonely childhood at boarding school. She went directly to the Ladies' Lounge, aware of the eyes of the cloakroom attendant and the maître d' staring after her, assessing the value of her four-year-old tweed suit and the matching coat from which she had removed the matted fur collar.

In the scented warmth of the lounge Kathryn checked her general appearance and her make-up. She looked neat but not striking, she decided; both her training and her own preference made her conservative.

"This is what he will see across the table in a few

minutes," she thought anxiously. A tall girl, thin, with good bones; the face narrow—well-bred but not beautiful. She frowned. The new hat she had recklessly purchased yesterday, to be worn for this luncheon, suddenly seemed wrong with the tweed coat—too bright, too frivolous. It had been an extravagance, but she had been sure that Don was going to make a formal proposal today, and Kathryn felt she could not bear to be proposed to in a brown felt hat that was two years old. So what if she had to do without desserts for a while? How often does a girl get an offer of marriage? She rallied her courage as she pulled the silly hat further to one side of her heavy knot of hair. Don was always telling her to get it cut, but she had a secret image of it covered by a soft white veil, and, later, of its shining dark length falling richly over a satin negligee. . . . No, she really didn't want to cut it. It was her one beauty.

She felt a thrill at the thought of marrying Don. She'd met him at a large party given by one of her old school friends. When he heard her name, he had seemed interested. That evening, he had asked her to go to an art show with him. In the next few weeks they had several dates, usually for concerts or opening nights of Broadway shows where they'd be sure to see "the right people." Don often explained to Kathryn how important it was for him to meet the right people.

He'd talked about marriage several times, but never definitely asked her. Kathryn understood that many young men didn't make formal declarations—just took it for granted that the woman of their choice would be willing. Donald had mentioned how valuable a prudent marriage to a woman of good connections could be for a man. Kathryn, incurably honest, warned him that her father's cousins had never paid much attention to her. In fact, since the death of both her parents in a car accident, she had hardly seen the wealthy, socially prominent branch of the Hendrix family. Don laughed and told her that what she really needed was someone with finesse to teach her how to get on in the world. He was always talking about ways to get on in the world. It made her a little embarrassed sometimes. Still, perhaps he was right. He had certainly made an unusual success of his own work. Kathryn knew nothing about the brokerage business, but Don's salary was many times what she herself earned in her secure, if unexciting, job in the library.

She glanced at her watch, then, startled, looked again. She'd been in the lounge fifteen minutes! She hurried out into the lobby, hastily checking the people who were standing waiting for a table. Only a few people had braved the cold, blustery November day. Don wasn't among them.

At twelve-thirty, Kathryn was the only person left standing in the lobby. The maître d' approached her. "You are waiting for someone, madame?"

"Mr. Donald Madson," Kathryn tried to put confidence in her voice. "Obviously he's been delayed. Has he reserved a table?"

He hadn't. "Perhaps madame would care to be seated until her escort arrives?"

"Oh, yes," said Kathryn thankfully.

He led her to a small table near the wall. It occurred to Kathryn that perhaps he just wanted her shabby coat out of his elegant lobby. She tried to concentrate on the menu, but her eyes kept straying to the entrance in the hope of seeing Don's trim figure. Twice a waiter came to take her order. The second time there was something in his manner which Kathryn found offensive. She had noticed a phone jack on the wall.

"Please bring me a telephone," she asked. The waiter did so and, to her discomfort, lingered nearby. She called Don's office.

The familiar voice of the receptionist sounded. "Barweed and Stone, Investments. May I help you?"

"Let me speak to Mr. Madson, please," Kathryn said.

"I'm sorr-ee, Mr. Madson is in conference."

"I must speak to—" Kathryn began.

The line went dead.

With the waiter's eyes upon her she dialed again, her fingers clumsy with nervousness and anger.

"Barweed and Stone, Investments. May I help you?"

"This is Miss Hendrix. Mr. Madson arranged to meet me for lunch at the *Rive Gauche*. I've been waiting an hour. Has something happened to delay him?"

Now it would be all right. The silly girl would remember that Donald had asked her to phone and tell Miss Hendrix he'd be delayed.

"I'm sorr-ee. Mr. Madson left half an hour ago with a client. He didn't say where he was going. May I take a message?"

Kathryn replaced the reciever on its cradle slowly. *Get out of here quickly,* her mind urged. *How could Don do this to me!* her heart protested. Humiliation and anger churned like opposing tides, confusing her thinking.

"M'sieu has been delayed?" smirked the waiter.

Somehow Kathryn managed to gather up her gloves and handbag, push back the chair and walk to the door. She knew that everyone in the small, glittering room was staring at her, commenting, amused or perhaps pitying.

Out on the busy street she looked again at her watch. Even if she walked back to the library, she'd be in plenty of time for work. . . . Then her whole body rebelled. She'd hinted about the purpose of this date to her superior in arranging for an extra hour off; she'd been coy and mysterious with her fellow-workers, answering their interested inquiries about the new—and unsuitable!—hat. She *could not* face their curiosity. Physically sick with disappointment, Kathryn boarded a bus that went in the opposite direction to the library.

The bus wasn't crowded. Kathryn took a seat beside a window on the left-hand side of the bus. The vehicle jerked and swayed its way along beside the curb. Kathryn stared, unseeing, at the passing traffic, her mind drearily shuffling through the possible explanations for Don's conduct.

Suddenly her eye was caught by the scarlet flare of a small elegant foreign car. A red light was momentarily holding the open car beside the bus. Driving it, dressed in matching scarlet, was a laughing, dark-haired girl, an exotic little creature whose gloved hands were competent on the wheel. She was turned in Kathryn's direction as she made some laughing comment to the man seated beside her. The man—

It was Don!

Kathryn could not mistake the small, compact body, the dark hair sleekly waved, the small ears set so neatly against the head. She had been seeing that face in her romantic visions for months. Involuntarily Kathryn beat her fist against the window of the bus in a gesture part greeting, part challenge.

"Don!" she called, and rapped sharply on the windowpane to get his attention. "*Don!* It's *me*, Kathryn!"

The girl driving the car glanced up, caught perhaps by the flash of movement of Kathryn's hand. Her eyes, big and dark, rested for a moment on Kathryn's face, then returned to the street. The red light had changed to green. As Kathryn watched, the girl made some remark and gestured toward the bus. Don flashed one quick glance over his shoulder, turned back, and shrugged. The red car shot away. The bus lumbered after it like a wallowing sea cow.

Kathryn fell back against the seat. At her shoulder, a fat woman breathing chili and garlic made a comment. "Somebody you knew? Prob'ly couldn't hear you, what with all the traffic."

Unable to find words to answer, Kathryn got up and pushed blindly past the well-intentioned woman. She had to get out *now*. She felt that everyone in the bus was speculating on her behavior, perhaps laughing at her. She reached the front entrance and waited for the bus to stop at the next light. The driver didn't open the door.

"Out!" Kathryn said sharply.

The driver grunted and swung the door open. Kathryn stumbled to the curb and began to walk along the street. Boisterous gusts of wind whipped at her, battered and jostled her, caught the tears that were flowing down her cheeks. Don's client, the person who had been even more important than a date made with Kathryn, was a beautiful girl—young, poised, obviously wealthy. She has everything, Kathryn thought miserably, while I had only—Don . . .

To escape the buffeting wind, Kathryn turned almost blindly into a side street. The district was unfamiliar to her—but the more unfamiliar, the better. Here in this rather dingy neighborhood she would not be likely to meet anyone she knew—anyone who would wonder why Kathryn Hendrix was crying on the street in broad daylight. She walked rapidly, head bent against the icy cold. In a few moments she noticed the first drops of rain. Before she could more than register the fact, the downpour was on her. The wind whipped sharp needles of sleet into her face, down her neck, against her legs. Kathryn raised her head to look around her. Was there a bookstore, a coffee shop—anywhere to take shelter?

The street was lined with old houses, neatly kept up but far from stylish. A few small stores, intruding on the houses, revealed that this was a neighborhood in transition. The rain came down harder.

"My new hat will be ruined," Kathryn thought. But what did it matter? Who was to see it, who to care? Still, she would be more than foolish to risk a bad cold. She had her job to think of—the job she would have to keep for the rest of her life. She looked around for some temporary refuge from the storm. A flash of brilliant color caught her eye. A small store had a painting on display in its single window. Stretched above both door and window, a sign proclaimed that this was the Moderan Gallery.

The picture which had caught her attention represented a sun-drenched Italian fishing village, with little pastel houses spilling crazily down the steep hillside to a smiling blue bay. And flowers everywhere—on roofs, hanging from outside stairways and windows, flourishing along the edge of the sand near the cliff. Without another thought, Kathryn turned into the gallery.

The interior was at first disappointing. Rows of cheap plywood screens held canvases of different sizes: seascapes, landscapes, portraits. The wooden floor was scarred and rather dirty. The light was poor. Kathryn was wondering whether she wanted to wait in this depressing place until the rain stopped, when a lighted portrait on the back wall caught her eye. She moved toward it, as much from reluctance to go back into the storm as from any desire to examine the picture.

It was a full-length portrait of a woman in elaborate eighteenth century costume. The first impression was of warmth and brilliant light. The dress was golden satin, the skirt extravagantly wide with ruffles of heavy gold lace on the overdress, and more lace and jeweled flowers embroidered on the bodice and underskirt. The bodice was cut revealingly low, exposing rounded flesh whose tones of apricot and cream had been stroked onto the canvas with obvious admiration by the artist. The woman's hair, built to a ridiculous height in the fashion of the late seventeen hundreds, was a blaze of titian red, so crimped and puffed and bejeweled that it seemed an artificial headdress rather than a woman's hair.

And then Kathryn raised her eyes to the face.

The woman had the most arrogantly beautiful countenance she had ever seen. Sensuality pouted in the full lips, pride flared in the exquisite curl of the nostrils, and the eyes—Kathryn felt a shiver of emotion ripple along her flesh as she met the challenge of those strange, light green eyes framed in long black lashes. The eyes caught hers, held them . . .

Deliberately Kathryn forced herself to look away, telling herself she wished to know who had painted this very life-like portrait—refusing to admit that the bold, pale green stare had frightened her. Near the foot of the portrait, where the painted pattern of a rich Turkish carpet served as a background, the artist had scrawled his signature: Adrian Bart. Kathryn had never heard of him, yet she thought that if he had painted many pictures as disturbingly alive as this one, the world should surely have been aware of his name. All the time she was bending to decipher the signature, Kathryn felt the pull of those arrogant eyes above her.

Adrian Bart had employed a technique which Kathryn had heard of, painting the eyes of his subject so they seemed to follow the viewer wherever he went. Reluctantly Kathryn looked up and met the green eyes a second time.

Now she was sure of it. That hard, mocking stare was evil. It was putting some kind of spell on her—drawing her ... Kathryn moved back a few steps involuntarily, putting distance between herself and the portrait. It was then she noticed a card tacked to the wall beside the picture frame.

LADY NADINE ELSINGHAM
by Adrian Bart
1774

and in smaller letters: "On loan from the Merlin Galleries, London."

Irresistibly the shallow green eyes drew Kathryn's glance. So alive, so insolent they were! What kind of female had she been, this titled Englishwoman in the absurd costume? Kathryn tried to overcome the effect of the eyes by laughing at the archaic dress and absurd hair style of the subject. She found she could not keep her eyes from the other woman's face. She gave in and fastened her own gaze on the green eyes that seemed to be drawing her, drawing ... There was a moment when she felt dizzy, faint—when the dirty floor seemed to shift beneath her feet—the very world turned—

"It can't be an earthquake!" she heard herself say, and then ...

She was standing on a deep-piled Turkish carpet. Instead of the bleak gray half-light of the Moderan Gallery, a warm yellow glow filled the air around her.

She lifted her eyes to the portrait— Yes, thank goodness, it was still there in front of her, the green eyes seeming brighter in the exquisite, evil face. And then she glanced down—and the world whirled around her again. Incredibly, insanely, she was dressed in a copy of that extravagant golden satin costume. Gasping in the heated air, Kathryn stared wildly around her.

She was standing on a square platform—a landing half-way up a staircase. On either side of her, wide, richly-carpeted stairs swept up to a railed gallery. Everywhere candles burned in lustered holders and sconces, providing the mellow light she had noticed. Gold-framed paintings hung on the silk-paneled walls. A huge bowl of flowers graced a table in front of the portrait. This was not the picture gallery! How had she come to this place? Who had put this costume on her?

Kathryn caught a flash of movement at the edge of her vision. She glanced up at the railed gallery. A woman, tall, gaunt, dressed all in black even to the cap closely framing her face, was staring down from the shadows of a pillar above. There was a rigidity—almost an agony of purpose—in her posture. At her shoulder stood a slender man whose dark hair fell across his forehead in casual disarray. Kathryn glimpsed the whiteness of his hand on the woman's dark sleeve. Then they moved back out of sight. There was a furtive air to their behavior.

But—this was *madness!* Kathryn turned and looked down the broad central stairway that led into a spacious, beautifully furnished hall. At the front door, a footman in a powered wig was ushering in a tall man, taking his hat and cape obsequiously. The man turned his head, his hair shining gold in the candlelight, and saw Kathryn.

He came forward politely a few steps, and sketched

14

a bow, but there was no smile of welcome on his face. He said coolly, "Admiring your portrait, milady?" and made to enter one of the rooms which opened off the hallway.

"Wait!" Kathryn stretched out a hand to him. Her mind was in wild confusion, striving to understand the situation in which she found herself, to make some kind of rational pattern out of the unbelievable reports of her senses. Somehow she had the conviction that this man, with his hard level gaze now meeting hers directly, would be a rock and a refuge for anyone lucky enough to be his friend. Was there something familiar about his face? The mouth, strong yet sensitive; the forehead, broad; the chin, decisive; the eyes arrogant beneath level brows—a strong man, not easily deceived. If he would help her . . .

"Where am I?" she faltered. "What am I doing here?"

The man frowned suddenly and began to turn away.

"Please! You *must* help me!" Kathryn took a step forward, catching the look of surprise and, yes, *dislike* on the man's face. Abruptly the surprise changed to alarm. For Kathryn was falling . . . falling down the strange, beautiful stairway . . . into blessed darkness.

Two

When Kathryn came to her senses, she was being carried along a beautifully furnished corridor in the arms of the golden-haired man. She stared over his shoulder, trying to orient herself. Marble statues and urns of fresh flowers were set in niches; candles blazed on the silk-paneled walls. Kathryn's cheek rested against a strong shoulder covered with cloth of dark blue material. She attempted to move, and a sharp agony went through her arm. She gasped. Through a fog of pain she heard the man's voice.

"You have hurt your arm, ma'am. It will be best if you lie quiet. I'll have you to your abigail in a moment."

'Abigail'? Kathryn raised her eyes to the man's face. Yes, it was the same golden-haired man who had entered the door just before she fainted. He was glancing down at her. Beneath a wide forehead, clear gray eyes watched her steadily. His face was handsome in a strong, masculine way: firm-lipped, firm-jawed. A newly-healed scar crossed his left cheek. Kathryn became aware that his features were set in an expression of controlled dislike. Dislike? But Kathryn had never seen him before. Why should he dislike her? And then the full terror of the situation swept over her, and she shut her eyes with an involuntary moan of shock.

The big man's arms tensed. "Have I hurt you? I am sorry for it," he muttered.

"No, it isn't that! You're very gentle!" Kathryn protested. "It's just that I'm so frightened—I can't understand any of this—" Her voice faded. The man turned into a doorway which was being held open by a flustered serving maid.

"You missed your footing at the landing, ma'am, and fell down the stairway," the big man said quietly. "You have hurt your arm. I have sent for the doctor. I'll leave you with your woman now." He deposited Kathryn on a bed whose feather-softness enveloped her with a treacherous lack of support. Then he stood back, looking down at her. "I trust you will be more comfortable soon." His voice seemed to Kathryn to hold wariness, a purely formal sympathy. *As though we were enemies,* she thought, with a flash of insight.

"When the doctor has seen you, I shall talk to him about your fitness to attend the reception tonight. I'll leave you now—"

"Oh, please, don't go!" In spite of his obvious dislike of her, Kathryn felt that his strength was the only reality she could cling to in this nightmare. "Please— just for a few minutes..."

The pain swept over her again, a sickening wave,

18

and she sank back defeated into the musty-smelling feather bed. But her appeal had not been useless. The big man, frowning slightly, returned to stand beside her. He said quietly to the hovering servant girl, "Bring her ladyship's dresser here at once. And light more candles."

As the girl ran from the room, the man's golden head bent over Kathryn. "Is the pain very great? What can I do for you?"

Kathryn drew a deep, shuddering breath, caught desperately at her reeling senses. "It isn't the pain so much," she began, holding her voice steady with a real effort of will. "It's this house—the portrait, this body—" She shuddered, looking down at the full swell of bare breast from which rose to her nostrils a gagging odor of musky perfume. She stretched the uninjured arm out to him in involuntary appeal.

And then she really saw the arm. The hand was covered with too many ornate rings, and the nails and knuckles were grimy. "It's dirty! This hand is dirty!" she wailed, made childish by shock and pain and terrible confusion.

The man continued to frown, but his voice was controlled and soothing. "The shock of falling, ma'am, and the pain of your arm, have disoriented your senses for the moment," he said. "Rest quietly until Dr. Anders comes. He'll give you something to make you feel better." It was the tone a conscientious adult would use to a sick child.

Kathryn shook her head wearily against the pillows.

"You don't understand," she said. "How could you? I can't accept any of this myself. Where am I? Is this some kind of nightmare . . . hallucination? I don't know what's happened to me!"

19

With the enforced patience of one humoring a fretful child, the man asked, "Just what is it you don't understand, Nadine?"

Kathryn's eyes flew wide open. "'Nadine'? That's not my name! I'm Kathryn!"

"What new trick is this?" The man drew back from the bedside, the expression of dislike clear on his face. "I warn you, Nadine: I meant what I said this morning. I have had more than I can stomach of your shifts and wiles. I can hardly believe that you would risk serious injury to try to change my mind—but in any case, it is useless. You leave for Brionny Keep in three days. Taking whomever you please with you," he added, an angry note in his voice.

Kathryn drew a deep breath. She was dizzy with pain and shock; her head seemed to be hollow and her body, to make matters worse, began to whirl in a vertigo she could not control. But she must think clearly. Her reason was at stake. The big man was openly hostile now. He was the enemy of this woman whose body she so frighteningly was wearing. Yet his steady eyes were honest and trustworthy, and his arms had been gentle and strong. Kathryn made a last effort. Her voice came out weaker than she expected, but she did speak, holding his eyes desperately with her own.

"For God's sake, sir—help me! I'm Kathryn Hendrix of New York City. I work in a library . . . I was looking at that portrait in a little gallery . . . and then I was here—" Her voice failed and she sank, still fighting desperately, into blackness.

What followed was an extension of the nightmare, with brief waking periods of too-bright lights and physical pain alternating with blackouts. The big man was almost always there in the background. Kathryn's eyes sought for him in a panic whenever she was conscious, and she heard her voice pleading with him to help her, and insisting that she was KATHRYN Hendrix.

At one point she awakened to see a black-robed woman bending close above her. The mask-like face, its flat black eyes hooded under heavy folds of flesh, was staring down fixedly at her. Where had she seen that intent and rigid stare? Yes! The woman had been watching her from the shadows of the pillar when this nightmare began! It was she! There was something in those inhuman empty eyes which utterly terrified Kathryn. She screamed in fear until someone came and took the woman away.

After a period in which time stretched and telescoped unbelievably, Kathryn found herself, her shoulders supported, sipping at a cup of bitter fluid. It was being administered by a competent-looking man in a dark coat and an odd white neckcloth something like an ascot.

"You're in costume, too," Kathryn said, smiling at him. "We're *all* in costume! Is it a masquerade?" She giggled. *I'm tipsy,* she thought. *Isn't this brandy he's giving me?*

The doctor glanced up inquiringly at someone near the bed. Kathryn turned to look. It was the big golden-haired man. "It's you!" she said happily. "Thank you so much for staying. I'm not afraid when you're here."

"Lord Elsingham," the doctor said, "Lady Elsingham has suffered a broken arm, and a certain amount of shock which normally accompanies the pain. She also appears feverish. I must recommend that she remain very quietly in bed for at least a week, so the arm can mend and so I can observe the course of her malady. I shall come in every day to see how she goes on. I must admit, my lord, that I don't like this disorientation. It is not normal in the case of a simple bone fracture. Her

21

ladyship appears to be sickening with some disease."

He stood up and moved toward the other man. Kathryn strained to hear what they were saying.

"Is there someone reliable who can attend her ladyship?" the doctor asked. "She should not be left alone, either by night or day if she continues to be subject to this—delirium."

"You do not think she will be well enough to leave her bed for some time, Dr. Anders?" It was more a statement than a question.

"Definitely not," answered the doctor. He hesitated. "I understand that her ladyship had planned to visit her family's estate in Ireland shortly?"

"That is so," Lord Elsingham said, wondering angrily how much more was known of his private affairs, and from what source the information had come. "A more immediate problem, however, is that His Majesty has graciously accepted my wife's invitation to attend her reception tonight. The occasion was to be the showing of a new portrait, just painted, of Lady Elsingham. I shall have to go immediately to the palace to make our excuses."

The doctor nodded. "You may say that it is impossible for her ladyship to receive him. Tell His Majesty that we fear she may have a severe infection. That'll keep him away—" he caught himself, then continued soberly, "I'll not try to cozen you, my lord. Her ladyship may be in real danger. I cannot understand this persistent failure to know who she is. The threat may be—" He hesitated again, glanced sharply at Lord Elsingham.

"To her reason?" supplied the tall man.

The doctor nodded reluctantly. "This continued confusion as to her identity...It may be—must be—a symptom of some infection. I shall be in again to see her ladyship tomorrow morning. And if her condition worsens, send someone for me at once. Meanwhile, a competent woman must be in attendance upon your wife every moment."

Kathryn's mind was reeling. These men thought her delirious—or crazy! But this was a dream, wasn't it? An unusually vivid nightmare? Dredged up from her subconscious by the pain and humiliation of Don's rejection of her. A sort of wish-fulfillment-fantasy? The golden-haired man was speaking again. Kathryn fought the sedative the doctor had given her to hear and understand what was being said. It seemed prosaic enough.

"I'll see that your instructions are carried out," Lord Elsingham said. "And my thanks, Dr. Anders."

The doctor was at the bedroom door. He turned. "The woman attendant should not, I think, be my lady's dresser. The woman seemed to put her into a frenzy." He went out, closing the door behind him.

Lord Elsingham was frowning as his eyes met Kathryn's. He appeared to be moved by the pleading, the raw fear, which she could not control. He said, searching her face wearily with his eyes, "Is this another one of your ploys, Nadine? A trick to avoid being sent to Ireland?"

Wordlessly, Kathryn shook her head.

"I promise you," the man said, "I shall not change my mind. The documents of which I told you exist in my safe. You have no bargaining power. Your choice is the same: an ugly scandal, which will result in a public bill of divorcement, or your immediate removal to your home in Ireland, with a guaranteed allowance from my lawyers as long as you stay out of England. We've been over this so often—"

"Lord Elsingham," Kathryn said urgently. "You are

a man of education—an intelligent man. I think you are an enlightened man for—for your time. I must appeal to you as such..."

He was staring at her, surprise and perplexity in his expression. "Why do you persist in playing this new role? And who has schooled you to speak so differently?"

Kathryn took heart. At least she had caught his real attention, broken through the polite mask which he donned when he dealt with his wife. She paused, reaching frantically for the right words, the words which might hold his attention and convince him of the reality of this fantastic, incredible situation. She took a deep breath.

"This is literally, for me, a matter of life and sanity. May I ask for the favor of five minutes of your time— and an unbiased attitude of mind? I swear to you that this is not some trick played by a woman you have obviously come to dislike and distrust, probably with justice." She hesitated, suddenly terrified by the unbelievable situation in which she found herself. *Was she insane? Was* this whole nightmare the delusion of an unbalanced mind? No! She had to believe there was some other explanation. Perhaps this man could help her—even though it was clear to her that he regarded her as his enemy.

"As one human being to another—five minutes, Lord Elsingham? With your mind open and unprejudiced by whatever has been at issue between you and—Lady Elsingham?"

He was really puzzled now. The frown which had drawn his eyebrows together had deepened, but he came toward the bed, drawing a chair close, and sat down.

"As one human being to another. I cannot deny such an appeal."

Kathryn felt a surge of relief. At least the look of dislike had left his face momentarily, to be replaced by an expression of guarded interest. Kathryn clenched her hands together in a gesture of intense concentration. "Let me begin by asking you to listen to—a story." Ignoring his small movement of protest, she went on quietly. "A woman had just received a painful blow to her self-image. The man she had confidently expected would propose marriage to her had revealed his lack of interest in the most humiliating way possible. The woman, blind with pain, wanders down an unfamiliar street in the rain. She takes shelter from the storm in the only available haven, a small art gallery. The woman enters. She sees a portrait. It depicts a woman, very beautiful but arrogant and—evil. The woman who has been rejected is . . . plain and without glamor. She is fascinated by the confident eyes of the painted figure. She cannot break away from the challenging green gaze which seems to follow her and—compel her attention. She experiences a sudden overpowering dizziness . . . falls . . . and finds herself in a strange house, dressed in the garish, shameless gown worn by the woman in the portrait. She is no longer in New York— worse, *she is no longer in her own body*, but seems to be caught in the living body of the woman whose portrait she had been looking at."

Kathryn paused, and searched the set face of the man with imploring eyes. Incredulity, impatience, rejection—she could read these in his expression.

At length he said, "Do you wish me to make a rational comment on this—story?"

"No, not yet," Kathryn hastened to say. "You promised me five minutes—and no prejudice!"

"Go on," he said after a minute.

"In addition to this nightmare change," Kathryn said quietly, "I—that is, the woman of whom I speak—

fell and broke her arm. She was carried to a bedroom by a man whose eyes were kind, although he obviously disliked the woman he was helping. Now, injured, terrified, in a strange place and what was undoubtedly a different time..." Kathryn held her clenched hand against her trembling lips, fought to regain her poise. So much depended upon this—so very much! And his eyes seemed coldly contemptuous. "Lord Elsingham! I am Kathryn Hendrix of New York City. And the date I saw on my calendar, when I went to work in the Uptown Library yesterday morning, was November five, 1974. *As God is my witness!"*

"Nadine, I must beg you to excuse me," Lord Elsingham said coldly. "I'll send your woman to you at once. Dr. Anders would be very angry with me for permitting you to excite yourself in this manner." He stood up.

Sudden anger flared in Kathryn's frightened heart.

"How dare you treat another human being with such arrogance, such prejudice? If you are a fair example of the intelligent Englishman, it's no wonder George the Third lost the Colonies!"

He halted, turned back to face her.

"What new nonsense is this? We haven't lost the Colonies."

"You're going to—in 1775."

Lord John hesitated, obviously torn between interest and contempt. "I apprehend you are referring to the Boston Tea Party and the subsequent closing of the Port of Boston by Parliament? Let me congratulate you—on your newly-acquired political expertise, ma'am. I had not realized you were a bluestocking! But you have your dates incorrect. Let me remind you that the petty disaffection in Boston occurred over a year ago, in 1773."

"War will be declared in 1775," Kathryn retorted hotly, still warmed by anger at his unfairness, "and ended by treaty in 1783 with a victory for the United States of America!"

"1783? Eight years in the future?" Elsingham didn't even try to understand the intense emotional response he was experiencing. He hated and despised this beautiful lying woman—didn't he? He had only contempt for her tricks, however disturbing and inventive they were becoming. Not once but many times bitten, he would be forever shy of her! So, suppressing the surprise and interest he felt at this unusual tactic, he said, "Doing it rather too brown, ma'am! Can it be that you hope to change my mind? Let me assure you that my decision is firm. I will not be taken in by this farrago of nonsense about 'United States' and insurrections. You Irish are all too ready to raise the flag of rebellion! You will leave London for Ireland as soon as you are well enough to travel. I cannot permit you to remain here, dishonoring my name with your public displays of wantonness, for eight more years while we wait for proof or disproof of your ridiculous statements."

He stared at her, reluctantly admiring, held against his will and better judgment by her beauty and the dramatic story she had told. Then he laughed angrily. "You're a clever devil, Nadine! You almost had me believing— Politics? That's a new start for you. You must have acquired a politically-minded lover—or one with a taste for government. My compliments on his skill as a tutor!" His fingers touched the newly-healed scar on his face. "Will he follow you to Ireland?" Then, when Kathryn, silent with despair, did not reply, Lord John continued, surprised at his own violence, yet unable to prevent the words, "I suppose we are to bid adieu to your young artist who has run tame in my

27

house this two months! How disappointing for him that he should be superseded at the moment of his triumph!"

With an ironic bow, Lord John left the bedroom.

Kathryn put her hand to her tear-wet face. "Am I mad? Oh, God, what is happening? Is this delirium—or am I really living in England—in the year 1775?"

Desperately she pulled together her disordered wits. There must be a rational explanation. Was she experiencing a nervous breakdown? She had been deeply shocked, wounded, by the cavalier treatment she had received from Donald Madson. But surely that would not have been enough to cause this kind of hallucination? Perhaps her soaking in the icy rain had given her a fever—but so soon? Or was this a virus infection, strengthened by nervous tension and exposure . . . ? Was she in a hospital, suffering fever and delirium? There was some comfort in the thought. Kathryn focused her eyes on the elegantly-furnished bedroom. Surely an elaborate fever dream! Even her wealthiest school friends, who had occasionally asked her to visit at their homes, had never boasted such a room.

The walls were paneled in pale green satin framed in white wood. The hangings were made of the same satin, draped back over sheerest white net with golden cords. The carpet, deep-piled, was a silky pale green. Charming gilt and satin lounging chaises were set on either side of a white marble fireplace, in which now gleamed and danced a cheery fire. Heavy crystal bowls of hothouse flowers perfumed the air. And everywhere there were mirrors—gold-framed, ornate, large, small, round, rectangular. This was the bedroom of a woman who worshipped her own beauty.

As she studied the room, Kathryn heard the door open quietly. She glanced quickly toward it, hoping against reason that Lord Elsingham had returned to discuss her situation. Entering the room was the same gaunt, black-clothed woman whose eyes had so terrified Kathryn during the time the doctor had been setting her arm. Kathryn drew the bed covers up to her chin in a futile effort to protect herself from that flat black gaze.

At the woman's shoulder was the same slender, dark-haired man who had stood behind her in the railed gallery. Very furtively now he followed the woman into the bedroom, shutting the door softly behind him. The two advanced toward Kathryn's bed.

"Who are you? What do you want?" Kathryn stammered. "Go away! I am sick!"

The gaunt woman stood near the bed, scanning her face intently. Without taking her eyes from Kathryn, she addressed the young man. "Something's amiss," she muttered. "The drug was not to have such an effect. I may have given her too heavy a dose—"

"Damn you and your devilish potions," snarled the man. "Didn't I warn you against it? I could have won her to me without your messes! You've driven her out of her senses, you damned old hag! What good is she to either of us in this state?"

"Keep your voice down," the woman commanded. "D'you want to bring the household on us? Have you forgot I've already been sent away by his high and mighty lordship? How long do you reckon you'll last around here if she's gone mad?"

The young man peered angrily at Kathryn. "Well? Has she?"

Kathryn pulled herself together. "I have told you to leave my room. Do I have to summon help to have you put out?" Her eyes went to the heavy bell-rope which dangled by the head of the bed.

The man drew back, alarm on his pale, handsome face. The woman was made of stronger stuff. She adopted an attitude of wheedling servility.

"Come, now, milady, you're not angry with old Donner, surely? Her that's been nurse an' maid an' dresser to ye since ye were a slip of a girleen, running hey-go-mad on the lovely green turf of home? 'Tis only a distempered freak you're feelin', from the pain in your blessed arm. Let Donner give you a potion, dearie. 'Twill do ye more good than all that silly doctor's quackery—"

Kathryn made a convulsive lunge at the bell-rope. Cursing under her breath, the young man leaped to prevent her. But Donner only smiled.

"Let her do it, ye cowardly scut. Sure an' it'll completely convince her fine lordling to put her away, if he's informed by his top-lofty London servants that his lady's entertaining her painter-boy in her bedchamber!"

Kathryn drew back her hand. Donner grinned. "That's better, milady. Now suppose you just let old Donner give ye a little draught to calm your nerves, like always?" She drew a small brown clay bottle from the pocket of her dress and began to uncork it. "Off to sleep we go, childeen. Donner'll have everything right by the time you wake."

The young man scowled at the servant. "What damned double game are you playing, you witch? I believe you've been scheming the whole time to get her sent back to Ireland, to Brionny Keep, where you can queen it over the peasants and run the castle and her ladyship too!"

Donner grinned evilly at him. "Well, little man? And what's wrong with that?"

"There's nothing in it for me—that's what! I've no

wish to cool my heels in a broken-down Irish castle, consorting with ignorant bumpkins! Damn it, woman, I was to have been presented to the King this very night! And now all's lost!"

Donner looked at him. "Get you gone, then, fancy man. You served to amuse milady and to disgust her fine lordling, but I've no further use for you. Run along with you!"

The artist glared at her, cast a humid, languishing glance at Kathryn, said, "Nadine? Beloved, is there no hope—?" Then, when Kathryn did nothing but watch him with fear and disgust, he sighed theatrically, turned, and made an exit whose dramatic value was marred by the extreme stealth which he employed in slipping out of the room. Donner sniffed.

"A pretty little man, and had his uses, but we're well rid of him. There'll be many a handsome buck eager to pay court to you when I have you safe back home, childeen."

"I am not going anywhere with you. I intend to remain in this house until I can straighten out this madness—"

Donner interrupted her. "'Madness'?" she repeated. "Now there's a word I'd be chary of tossing around, milady. You'll maybe have heard of Bedlam, and the loonies they keep there, chained up to make a show for the fine folk you've been flouting this last year? Are you anxious for them to come and vent their spite on you, and you in the cold cell amidst the filth?"

Kathryn stared at her with horror. *Bedlam*? She had indeed heard of the Hospital of Saint Mary of Bethlehem in London, where the mentally ill were confined in degrading conditions, the worst of which, to Kathryn's mind, was the practice of selling tickets to watch the wretched madmen as though they were beasts in a zoo. "You wouldn't—you *couldn't*—!"

"'Tis not I but that stiff-rumped lordling you've out-raged so freely this twelvemonth who'll commit you. Think you your fine husband would lift a finger to save you? Not after the duel he had to fight with Lord Beltane, and nearly killed the poor man for his comments about the lovely Lady Elsingham. Lord Johnny will jump at the chance to be rid of you and all his troubles ended—"

Kathryn shrank back in horror. Donner, sure of her victory, adopted a coaxing tone. "Be reasonable, chil-deen. Take the easy road. Let's off to Brionny Keep as his lordship wishes. You'll have plenty of money, for he's far from a miser. You'll be happier there, I promise you!"

"I cannot leave this house," whispered Kathryn, staring straight in front of her with haunted eyes. "It's the only link I have with—the future! No, go away!" she almost shouted, as Donner came closer. "Can't you see what you've done? I'm not Nadine Elsingham! I'm Kathryn Hendrix!"

"One little sip of this and all your troubles will be over," promised the woman grimly. Kathryn stared at her with horrified revulsion. There was an ancient evil around her, a cesspool stench. Donner seized Kathryn's arm and pulled her closer. The rough grasp sent a searing agony from wrist to shoulder of the broken arm. But the pain was nothing to the fear, the horror which threatened to overwhelm her. She knew in that moment that she must not traffic with this creature of the power of darkness. Frantically she struck at the woman with her free hand, sending the small brown bottle flying. Donner cursed at her, a foul string of vicious filth.

"Go away!" Kathryn screamed.

Whatever else Donner might have done was prevented by a stern voice from the doorway. "Donner, his lordship gave orders you were not to enter her ladyship's room again. No," as Donner began to protest, "don't make excuses. With my own ears I've just heard her ladyship order you away. Must I call a footman?" The speaker shook her head, reducing Donner's outburst to the level of a naughty child's tantrum. "Such a commotion as this isn't at all the thing in an English gentleman's establishment, whatever may be the custom in Ireland!" As she spoke, the newcomer was shepherding the nonplussed Irishwoman from the bedroom in much the fashion of a wise old sheep dog with a bad tempered old ewe. Then she closed the door gently and came toward the bed.

She was a plump little middle-aged woman, dressed neatly in a gray gown with a white muslin fichu and apron. She was obviously a superior servant, grown old in the service of milord's family, with the freedom of manner earned by years of faithful devotion. She spoke now in a tone of indulgent concern.

"Be easy, milady. Bennet won't let the nasty creature come near you again. What can I do to make your ladyship comfortable?"

Kathryn's taut nerves relaxed under the motherly attitude. She regarded this cheerful little woman with gratitude. Was this what it was like to have a mother? This sense of security and affection and hope? Kathryn's own mother had died when she was five. Boarding schools, however well recommended, do not fill the gaps left by the loss of a family.

"If I could just rest for a few hours...I am so weary...so confused..."

The little woman set about making Kathryn comfortable. In a few minutes the sheets were gently smoothed, the pillows plumped, the drapes drawn against the light, and a cool washcloth was moving refreshingly over Kathryn's heated face and neck.

"Oh, that's so good," she murmured. "Thank you, Mrs. . . . ?"

"I'm Bennet, your ladyship. You won't remember seeing me when first you came from Ireland, what with the excitement of the wedding and all. And of course you haven't seen me since, because I live down at Elsinghurst Village—that's in Master John's domain. My brother has a farm near the village. It was given to us when we came down from his lordship's estates in Scotland. I was brought down to be Master John's nurse," she chatted on cosily. She seemed to know exactly how to help a frightened sick girl to find her poise.

Kathryn felt herself drifting off into a relaxing sleep . . . *But she mustn't!* She jerked herself upright. "Bennet—I've got to think—plan—find a way out of this . . ." Then the hopelessness of trying to explain again the unexplainable came over her, and she began to cry. "He doesn't believe me, Bennet! Lord John doesn't believe me!"

"There, there, dearie," crooned the nurse, "Whether he does or he doesn't, he sent me to care for you. 'Do your best for her, Bennet,' he said to me before he left. 'She needs your help.' And he had his concerned look on his face the while. A very compassionate little fellow Master John was, as a child."

"But he seemed so angry—" faltered Kathryn. "Oh, Bennet, how can anyone believe my story when I can't even believe it myself? What am I going to do?"

"The first thing you're going to do is have a proper cup of tea—hot and sweet, to put strength into you. And then you'll tell Bennet what's the trouble, and we'll find a way out of it."

Kathryn's eyes were full of tears. "If we only could! If I could explain it all to you, and then you could tell Lord John— But you said he had left?" she asked, with a strange feeling of loss.

"Oh, yes, milady. His lordship had to rush away to wait upon the King, to explain why he couldn't entertain His Majesty tonight. He trusted me to see that you have whatever you need."

"Bennet—you don't understand. Lady Nadine is in deep disgrace . . . And I'm afraid no one can get me what I need." And she put her free hand on her burning forehead, as the tears flowed again down her cheeks.

"There, milady, have a nice cry," urged Bennet so indulgently that Kathryn felt a ridiculous desire to chuckle. "It'll do you good." She glanced toward the door. "I told one of the kitchen maids to bring up a pot of tea as soon as I rang." Suiting action to word, Bennet pulled strongly on the bell-rope. "Now we'll soon have you sipping a nice hot cup with plenty of sugar, and then a spoonful of the mixture Dr. Anders' manservant had just brought to the door as I came up—" She bustled over and set another log on the fire. Already the great bedroom felt safer, friendlier. "You'll soon feel much more yourself, milady."

Kathryn managed a weak and watery smile. "That's what I need, Bennet. To feel more like myself..." As she thought about the words, she found herself laughing and crying at the same moment. *Insane,* her shocked mind shouted, but the hysterical laughter went on.

Muttering her concern, Bennet hastened over to the bed and took the younger woman in her arms. For a few minutes she held the gasping, shaking body, patting, soothing, wiping away tears with a large clean handkerchief redolent of lavender. Kathryn, so exhausted she could scarcely think, surrendered herself to the gentle ministrations. Finally she murmured, "Bennet—if I could just have a hot bath! Would there be hot water, do you think?"

Bennet drew back, surprised. "With your injury, milady? It would be a most chancy proceeding."

"If you knew how dirty I feel—! I'm sure a warm bath would relax me and help me to rest. Please, Bennet?" she pleaded like a small child.

The nurse's face softened. "Well, milady, if you're all that set on it—I could give you a sponge bath, keeping you well covered against the draughts." She surveyed Kathryn doubtfully. "And your hair! Whatever heathen arrangement they've made of that pretty hair of yours! My fingers itch to get at it."

Kathryn gave a hopeful smile. "I *need* you, Bennet. It's as though you were *sent*. Please don't let them take you away from me."

Deeply touched, Bennet shook her head. "No one could. His lordship's orders are obeyed in this house."

"That isn't what I meant," Kathryn stammered. "People talk—terrible things are said..."

"I never listen to servants' gossip," said Bennet stoutly. Her eyes on the girl were steady and kind.

"But if it were true...or seemed to be so?" faltered Kathryn. "Bennet, I swear to you that I have never knowingly harmed his lordship or anyone in this—in this..." She broke off. It had been impossible to convince Lord John. How much more so would it be to prove to this devoted servant that her nursling's wife was in fact a woman from the future? She sighed. "Forget it," she said wearily. "Thank you, anyway."

Puzzled, Mrs. Bennet bustled about getting a table cleared for the tea-tray, and another set up near the bed with soap and cloths and big towels. "Where's that lazy girl with the tea?" she muttered, her worried gaze on the pale woman lying so listlessly in the bed.

As she spoke, there was a subdued kick at the door. Bennet opened it to admit a wide-eyed girl bearing a huge silver tray. She set it on the table Bennet pointed out, then listened open-mouthed to Bennet's quiet-voiced instructions. When the servant had gone, Bennet poured steaming tea into a fragile china cup, spooned in sugar, stirred, and brought the result to Kathryn.

"Drink this, milady. It will do you good."

Kathryn really didn't want it, but she sipped dutifully and then with rising enthusiasm. It was good. But then a disturbing memory from childhood reading surfaced in her mind: *"Neither eat nor drink in the land of faerie, lest you thereby close forever the way of return to your own place."* A shiver of fear passed through her body. *Superstition,* she mocked herself; foolishness! But the fear persisted. Bennet, watching her unobtrusively, thought she had never seen so despairing a look on a human face.

"Is the tea to your taste, milady?" she asked. Anything to change that hopeless look!

"Thank you, Bennet. It *is* good," Kathryn replied, and Bennet was somewhat comforted to see the younger woman trying to smile. Shortly the little kitchen maid returned with two large brass cans full of hot water. Bennet poured some into a bowl, then turned to Kathryn with a frown.

"Now, milady—are you sure you should make the effort?"

Setting her lips against the pain of her arm, Kathryn said, "I'm sure."

Bennet dismissed the servant, then gently, carefully, she got Kathryn out of the bewildering complexity of unfamiliar (to her) undergarments. Setting a pillow tenderly under the injured arm, Bennet gave the sponge bath efficiently, as she would have done to a child. She kept up a low-voiced commentary as she worked.

"You're that lovely, milady, 'tis no wonder half of London's talking...Tsk! tsk! what's that woman of yours thinking of? Your feet *are* grimy!...Oh, your poor arm! And your shoulder's bruised, too." She sighed. "Dr. Anders will be extremely annoyed with me if I've let you do yourself a harm, but you were right. You couldn't rest with that dirt on you!"

Kathryn chuckled weakly. "Bless you, Bennet! Just get me dry and covered up—and we'll neither of us breathe a word of this."

Bennet acknowledged the feeble joke with a smile. This girl had spirit and courage too. She was glad she hadn't permitted the other servants to gossip in her presence. There was something terribly wrong with Master John, she'd realized it two days ago when she arrived in London for her annual visit at the town house. She'd been ready to dislike the young wife who was apparently causing him so much trouble. But this forlorn child with the wide, frightened eyes—! Bennet thought surely there had been some terrible mistake. In spite of her attitude, she'd heard rumors, but this girl was no wanton, no virago. Bennet, feeling partisan, leaned over and tucked a fresh sheet carefully around the lovely body.

Kathryn looked up at her.

"Pray for me, Bennet," she whispered.

"Aye, that I will," Bennet said, much moved. "I'll just be a minute more, milady. I'll take the jewels and ribbons out of your hair, and those silly wires, and then

I'll give you the laudanum water Dr. Anders sent over. That'll put you to sleep—"

"A drug? Oh, *no!*"

"I'll be staying the whole night right here beside you, milady," Bennet promised. "Now take your medicine like a good child."

Smiling faintly, Kathryn drifted obediently into sleep, watching the glow of the firelight on the plump kindly face of Master John's nurse.

Three

Kathryn came slowly up out of the drugged sleep. She became aware of unfamiliar odors: the acrid tang of
woodsmoke and the heavy sweetness of hothouse flowers. And then comfortable sounds: somewhere near, an
open fire crackled cheerily, and a woman's voice was
humming softly a familiar lullaby. Eyes firmly closed
to retain as long as possible this unaccustomed sense
of luxury and ease, Kathryn stretched drowsily. She
felt a fullness and a warm immediacy of life in her
body. Even in this unusual relaxation, she was richly
aware. Usually when she woke to the shrill of the
alarm, it was with a sense of pressure and tension. Get
up, wash, dress, eat, catch the bus to the Library—don't
be late, don't catch cold, you can't afford to miss
work . . .

As the accustomed fears and tensions took over, depression like a groping gray fog sent its tendrils into her waking consciousness. There was something unpleasant she had to face—

Her growing unease was checked by the sound of a door opening and a deep voice speaking quietly.

"Good morning, Bennet. Still at your post, I see. This is not the pleasant vacation I had hoped to give you."

"No matter, my lord. I was pleased to be here with her ladyship."

There was a rustling of skirts, then the woman's voice, closer, subdued. "She's still sleeping. Isn't she the bonny one? The pain's been bad, I think. Her ladyship has been very restless in spite of the laudanum."

The deep voice showed concern. "Poor Bennet! You've had no rest at all, have you?"

"Master John, she touches my heart, the poor bairn. She's that fearful and thrawn—"

"Don't go all mystical Scot on me, Bennet," the man said with a teasing note in his voice.

"I mean it, sir. She's that terrified of something, she pleaded with me not to leave her. Like a child she sounded, frightened and alone. And she sent that Irish woman dresser of hers packing last night, and that artist fellow too. I know a little of what's been said, Master John, but her ladyship is not what they hint! She's—*innocent!*"

The man's voice hardened, became a little remote even with this trusted servant. "I wish you were right."

There was a brief silence. Kathryn waited in the comfortable lethargy of laudanum, hearing, yet not completely involved. This was a *very* interesting dream! She really ought to be up and getting ready for the cold bus ride to the Library, but surely just a few minutes more wouldn't hurt ... She had never had a dream so vivid—!

The man's voice, so deep it set up a little quiver of resonance in her body, was saying quietly, "Did her ladyship seem—rational to you, Bennet?"

There was a longer pause. A tiny needle of alarm thrust itself into Kathryn's calm. *'Rational'*? Whose rationality was being questioned?

The woman's voice came slowly, delightful with its hint of Scots' burr. "As to that, sir, ye'll ken I'm no authority. Her ladyship had the shock of a bad fall and a broken arm ... and then the drug from the doctor—"

"Stop hedging, Bennet," the man said sternly. "I know you have always been reluctant to speak ill even of people you don't like—but I *must know*—"

"She's nothing like I've been told, sir," the admission came reluctantly. Then, more firmly, "But that's to say nothing, Master John! Malicious tongues distort the truth, as I've told you often and often! This woman's like a wee bairn lost in the dark!"

Kathryn could hardly catch the man's next words, so low was his voice. "Would you say she was—mad, Bennet?"

'Mad'? But that meant—insane! Kathryn's eyes snapped open. This dream was turning into a nightmare.

No dream. She was lying in the lovely pale green and white bedroom she had thought was part of the dream. Near the four-poster stood the plump, sweet-faced woman servant of her dream, and beside her, the tall figure of the golden-haired man, elegantly dressed in the fashion of the late eighteenth century. It was the man who had caught her as she fell down the stairs.

43

Both these people were staring at her with worried faces. Kathryn stretched out her free arm toward them.

"Oh, please help me! I'm not insane! It's just a nightmare—a bad dream!" She struggled to sit up in the feather bed, giving her broken arm an agonizing twinge.

Bennet tutted worriedly and hurried over to support her shoulders. "Now, now, milady, you mustn't fash yourself..." She turned her head to the man. "You'd best be leaving us, sir."

"I'll send for Anders," Lord Elsingham began, but Kathryn cried out, "Please! Don't go away! Stay just for a moment. I must talk to you..."

His lordship moved reluctantly toward the bed. He superintended the placing of pillows behind Kathryn's shoulders so that she could face him sitting up, for which courtesy she felt deep gratitude. "Get her some hot chocolate, Bennet. And some bread and butter."

"Aye. That'll give her strength," agreed the woman. "I'll make it myself," and she hurried from the room.

Kathryn raised her eyes to meet Lord John's wary look. "Thank you for listening to me," she began with some difficulty. Her free hand was clutching the coverlet so tightly that her knuckles showed white, and the beautiful green eyes were wide with fear. His wariness gave way to compassion.

"Don't be afraid, ma'am. If you are ill, the best doctors shall treat you. A few months' rest in Ireland, and your memory will be restored."

Kathryn tried to smile her gratitude for his concern, but the situation was much too serious for anything but straight dealing. Hadn't she pleaded with this man before, begged his understanding, only to receive a crushing rebuff? What in God's name had the beautiful Nadine done to arouse in her husband such unrelenting

44

hostility? For Kathryn was forced to accept the reality of the situation at last. She was locked into the body of a beautiful woman who had lived two hundred years before Kathryn was born.

Lord Elsingham was staring at her with that look of wary hostility slightly tempered by concern. Obviously he was a good man, compassionate even where he could not trust. Could the truth, the integrity, in Kathryn reach out and convince such a man against all the evidence of his mind, memory, senses? The girl drew a deep, ragged breath and faced his challenging eyes.

She did not know that something in her manner, the agonized yet direct glance of her eyes, most especially her choice of language and the manner of her speaking—so different from those to which Lord John was accustomed, had created an unwelcome problem for him. He did not want to make any re-evaluation of his judgment about his wife. During the last year he had been hurt too often, too deeply, by the beautiful Irish termagant he had married. "Marry in haste; repent at leisure." Her abruptly changing moods, her outrageous displays of temper and bad manners in public, her licentious behavior, had burned too deeply. He had promised himself that never again would he be tricked by the exciting wanton who had been his wife for one tempestuous year. Thinking of the ugly scenes, the malicious rumors, the scornful laughter, his expression hardened.

Kathryn noticed the grimly-set jaw and her heart fell. For a minute he had seemed almost ready to accept her, to listen without bias. She hurried into speech with a sense that her cause was already lost. Deliberately she tried to make her language that of the 1970s. Oh, if only she knew more about the real Lady

45

Elsingham! She would perhaps be able to demonstrate that the mind within this beautiful body was not Nadine's.

"Sir," she began, low-voiced, "if I do not address you in the proper way, it is because for two hundred years my American countrymen have owed no allegiance to the British crown. We 'colonists,' as you called us, found your taxation without representation unbearable, and we fought you and finally defeated you with the help of France." Trying not to notice his frown, she hurried on. "I am only a librarian in New York's Uptown Library, not a history major—but I did go to Radcliffe College and my minor was American History—so I do know something about the details of the American Revolution of 1776-1783—"

"Very convenient." A rather scornful smile twisted his lips. "Since this is only the year 1775, no one will be able to verify your claims for some time. But at least you are remarkably consistent. Those are the dates you quoted me last night. There is coherence in your story . . ." *if nothing else,* his tone implied.

Kathryn's face whitened. She had lost him! Still she held her voice steady. "I have no defense against your suspicions, sir. And I am aware, believe me, that my statements are impossible to substantiate. I can only swear that what I tell you is the truth as I know it. Perhaps there is philosophical justification for the theory of alternate realities. What *I know* as reality is that I am Kathryn Hendrix, of the Barton Apartments, New York City; that my Social Security number is 565-48-4743, and *that,* as the American soldiers who fought in two world wars and two police actions could tell you, is all I am required to tell the enemy on capture: name, rank, and serial number."

The big man's eyes were the cold gray of a winter

sea. "I feel I must warn you against this game you are playing, Nadine. Dr. Anders was disturbed by your wild talk. He even hinted that he feared madness...For your own sake, lest your situation become worse, why not accept with good grace the fact that you have lost whatever game you are playing, and salvage what you can from the wreck of our marriage?"

Kathryn felt a sudden, irrational surge of pity for the tall, proud man standing before her. It was plain his wife had wounded more than his self-esteem. He must have loved his Nadine very deeply to have been so vulnerable to her actions. *As I thought I loved Don,* she reminded herself. Kathryn knew all about that pain!

Lord John was speaking in a steady voice. "You'll be happy in Ireland. I'll see to it that you do not lack for any luxury, so long as you live quietly and do not disgrace my name. Surely you can be discreet if it is to your advantage—"

Kathryn's head had begun to ache, and her arm was one solid throb of pain. She said wearily, "I can't convince you, can I? You aren't willing to give me a real test. Surely there must be something I can do that your Nadine could not? Mathematics? Languages? I was taught French and Latin, psychology, civics, library sciences...Question me! I'll do anything to convince you. Anything to get myself off the hook, as we say in 1974."

Lord John was frowning. Kathryn, searching for a way to hammer home her knowledge of the science of the future, went too far. "I'm not a physicist, but I know that in 1942 Dr. Fermi developed an atom bomb, and in 1969 the United States landed the first two men on the moon," she concluded proudly.

"You can't expect me to take this seriously? Atom

47

bombs and men on the moon? I don't believe in witch-craft. And you would be well advised not to let anyone hear you laying claim to such forbidden skills."

"Witchcraft? Is that what you think—?" began the girl, but Lord John interrupted, sternly.

"What else? Do you have some *rational* explanation for your claim of a miraculous flight through space and time *from the future?* On an 'atomic' broomstick, per-haps?"

Kathryn felt the surge of anger this man seemed capable of arousing in her. She said hotly, "That is unworthy of an educated man. I've read a great many romantic novels about the sense of justice and fair play so dear to the English, but apparently they were just that—romantic lies. You have a completely closed mind! You are what we call in my time a male chau-vinist pig! You're unwilling to listen to anything out-side your own narrow circle of belief—!"

Lord John's lips had set in a smile of cold distaste. He bowed ironically. "Congratulations, Nadine! It's re-assuring to see you restored to your normal sprightly temper. I'll leave you to rest and recuperate your strength—" Then, struck by the look of despair on her face, he said more gently, "Forgive me. You and I are fated to quarrel, are we not? But surely you've learned to know me well enough this past year to be sure I won't throw you out of the house with a broken arm, child. I won't send you to Ireland until it is mended, and your fever healed." He tried to smile. "Those novels you read must have been very exciting! Try to rest, Nadine. I'll speak to you again in a few days, when you have recovered from this—mental disturbance."

And he was gone from the room before Kathryn, startled by his change of manner, could find anything to say.

Four

Kathryn *might have* taken heart if she had been able to observe Lord John's behavior in the next few hours. Leaving instructions for her care with Bennet and the butler, he drove his curricle to the consulting rooms of Dr. Anders. He had a lengthy talk with that worthy, telling him exactly what his patient had said.

Dr. Anders shook his head soberly. "I don't like the sound of this, my lord, and that I'll tell you. Your lordship knows what would be the general opinion if such wild talk were to be repeated—"

"Then I trust you won't repeat it, sir," said Lord John.

"Of course I won't," the little doctor snapped. "Have I not been doctor to Elsinghams since before you were born? Is it likely I'd go nattering around the town with

49

a story sure to bring your lady into trouble?"

"I'm worried, Anders," confessed Lord John reluctantly. "She seems to be so *sure*—and she's different."

Anders pounced on that. "In what way?"

"Well, even Bennet—my old nurse; I've asked her to take care of Nadine—even Bennet remarked on her manner of speech. Since the accident it is different. She uses words I'd swear Nadine hadn't known. Her voice is softer, more musical," he grimaced in sudden embarrassment at the term, but went on steadily, "She has an accent, but it definitely is not the Irish brogue I once found so charming."

"So. Her ladyship speaks differently. What else?"

"She knows things Nadine didn't know about history—"

"But we have agreed that her ladyship is quite wrong about this war she claims has happened, have we not?" Anders reminded him.

Lord John frowned. "She says it's *going* to happen."

The other man's lifted eyebrows stopped him.

"We'll have to wait awhile to learn the rights of that, won't we, milord?" the doctor commented drily.

"Her talk of atomic bombs and space flight," persisted Lord John. "Isn't that significant? Nadine knew nothing and cared less for science in any form."

"But you did say her ladyship claimed to be a reader of romantic tales," the older man reminded him.

"Where would she have found such fantastical ideas as a landing of men on the moon? Not in my library!"

"That's where you're wrong, milord. Your father had a fine classical library, Greek and Roman authors, many translated into English. I recall him mentioning, over a glass of sherry, the day you were born, milord, one Lucian of Samosata, whose hero voyages to the moon. On the thrust of a waterspout, if I recall correctly," he ended with a smile. And in the face of the involuntary gesture of protest from Lord John, he continued firmly, "There is, however, a matter of more urgent concern which I must discuss with you, milord. Speaking of your father, you are very like him. A most impulsive man was Lord Harold, and overly quick to action."

Lord John's lips opened to make quick protest, and then shaped into a reluctant grin. "Doing it much too brown, Anders. My father was the most rigidly controlled—"

"Impulsive," repeated the doctor firmly, *"and* emotional. It hastened his end. Allow me to know: I was his personal physician for over forty years. Now, I shall expect you to receive the information I am about to impart to you with calm—or at least with control." He frowned at the younger man. "Early this morning, Mrs. Bennet sent a footman to me with a small brown clay bottle she had found on the floor of her ladyship's room, half-hidden by the bed-curtains. She felt I should know about it. It contained a drug—but not any drug which I had ever prescribed for her ladyship. I sent it to an apothecary to confirm my suspicions. I'll not worry you with its Latin name, milord, but tell you shortly that the little phial contained a most dangerous drug, whose continued use would be mind-destroying."

Lord John stared at him with a stunned expression. Then, "God!" he snapped. "Are you telling me that Nadine—"

"I am telling you nothing except that Mrs. Bennet says she found this near your wife's bed."

"Bennet wouldn't lie," said Lord John heavily. "Is this the reason for these wild tales of Nadine's?"

Dr. Anders regarded him sourly. "You jump to conclusions, milord. No one has suggested that her lady-

51

ship is in the habit of dosing herself with that foul muck."

"Then how—who—?"

"Bennet told me that your wife was put into considerable agitation at the presence of her dresser—"

"Donner!" shouted Lord John, and turned to leave the consulting room in haste.

"Lord John!" The doctor halted him. "Again you go too fast, milord. Nothing is yet proven. But we now have," he relented enough to admit, "some alternate speculations which may eventually lead us to the truth about this disturbing matter. My counsel at the moment is that you investigate quietly, first ascertaining the whereabouts of the woman Donner and placing her under close observation—"

"Too late," admitted his lordship wryly. "My cursed impulsive nature! I sent her packing yesterday."

The doctor pursed his lips. "You had better make sure she actually went."

"By God, I'll do that," promised his lordship grimly, and took his leave.

His second call was at the elegant lodgings of one of his two best friends, Mr. Randall Towne. That exquisite was entertaining the third member of their friendship, Lord Peter Masterson, at a belated breakfast.

Two less similar men would have been hard to find among London's *haut ton*. Randall was slender, dark-haired, volatile; Lord Peter appeared to be a lazy giant of a man, but his reflexes were amazingly fast, as his intimates had reason to know.

Randall greeted the new arrival with his usual high good humor. "What ho, Johnny! Whither away so early this fine morning—or is it afternoon?"

Lord Peter contented himself with a slow smile and a simple "Johnny."

Randall continued, "Draw a chair and have a bite of this ham. It's quite tolerable. And some ale, or coffee? I think there's some left."

Lord Peter was unobtrusively scanning his friend's face. Now he said quietly, "Do sit down, Johnny. Is something wrong?"

Lord John took a chair at the table and accepted a cup of coffee. He stirred it slowly. "I need—"

His friends waited.

"What?" prodded Randall, after a moment.

Peter kept chewing ham meditatively, his eyes on his friend.

John shrugged. "Help? Advice? Yes, perhaps that's the word. I need your advice."

The other two men exchanged wary glances.

"Lady Nadine hasn't—" began Randall.

"Only too happy—" Peter was saying at the same instant. Both stopped, disconcerted.

Lord John considered them for a moment, then said, "I shall have to confide in you. My—that is, Nadine— fell down the stairs yesterday and broke her arm—"

Randall broke in, "Have you forgotten, old chap? That's what you had us informing all your guests last night, while you were at the palace making your excuses to His Majesty."

"Needn't treat Johnny like the Village Idiot," murmured Peter, "even if he occasionally acts that way. He remembers what we did last night. This is probably something else. Why don't you let him tell us?"

Ignoring this exchange, John said, "The broken arm is the least of the troubles."

"You don't mean that painter feller—?" began Randall.

Peter silenced him with a frown. "Let him finish!"

"My wife tells me she is someone called Kathryn—" began Lord John.

"Catherine what?" interrupted the irrepressible Randall.

"What does it matter?" snapped John at the end of his patience. "We know her name is Nadine."

But Randall wouldn't accept this. "Much better to find out who she is. It could matter a great deal. I've known some pretty frightful Catherines in my time, old boy. I had a cousin, twice removed ...! And there was that shrew Kate in the *Taming* play—"

"Ignore his maunderings," advised Peter wearily, "or we'll never get to the problem."

John set his teeth. "I come here on a matter which is, to me at least, of great importance, and you clowns turn it into some kind of jest—"

"Not at all!" Lord Peter protested. "I was merely trying to silence this crowing cock so you could proceed."

"I'm not sure I've the stomach for it," said Lord John grimly. *"However*—! My wife further informs me that she lives in New York City, in America, and that she—" he hesitated, then concluded in a voice without inflection, "lives there in the year 1974."

Even the voluble Randall was struck silent.

After a pause, Lord Peter asked quietly, "And the doctor?"

John shrugged. "Observe—wait ... I don't know what to think. She—asked me to help her."

Randall exploded angrily. "Well, I know what to think! If you'll forgive me, or even if you won't, John, I'll tell you what *I* think!"

"Oh, Lord," murmured Peter.

"I think," persisted Randall angrily, "that she's play-

ing another of her tricks on you, John, and I wouldn't stand for it. The whole town's talking—"

"Am I to suppose, from that, that you have made all of London conversant with my private affairs?" asked Lord John, stiffly.

"You are to suppose no such thing, Johnny," corrected Peter. "Take a damper. This little cock crows loud, but never clucks a word about anything important."

"Well, thank you!" gasped the cock, much affronted.

Lord Peter continued, "You know we don't talk, Johnny, but as your closest friends, we—know how things have been..."

"Bound to," agreed Randall. "Peter was your second at that duel—"

Lord Peter ignored him. "How can we help you?"

Lord John shrugged, spread his hands.

Peter said slowly, "You loved her once, and she loved you enough to marry you—"

Randall sneered. "Fustian!"

"No, let him speak, Randy."

Peter continued quietly, "You say she is appealing to you for help on strange grounds. Surely if she were trying some trick, she would never have offered such an insane story. For one thing, it puts her at your mercy. With such evidence, you'd have no trouble putting her away under restraint."

"She knows that. And she sticks to her story." He got up and paced around the room. "She's different."

"In what way?" Randall was still suspicious.

"Her voice is changed and she uses a different vocabulary. It's—uncanny, hearing that voice from Nadine's mouth."

Peter got up and joined his friend at the window. "Would you like us to come around and speak to her?"

Randall frowned and shook his head at this rash offer, but Lord John accepted gratefully.

"Thank you, yes! You've both met Nadine, talked with her. Dr. Anders had never seen my wife before—she was never sick a day in her life—so he wouldn't notice a change even if there was one."

"We can't just go bursting into Lady Nadine's bedroom," objected Randall. Then he caught Peter's eye and blushed.

Peter spoke hastily. "We'll go tomorrow. Bring flowers and all that. Warn your people to expect us, Johnny."

Lord John smiled at him ruefully. "Thank you. I know you'll hate it, but I have to be sure. You see, Bennet says my wife's frightened—and innocent."

Randall's laugh grated harshly. "Tell that to someone who was not your second at the duel last month. Was it an innocent caused you to get that scar on your face?"

"Be quiet," commanded Lord Peter sternly. "We'll go, John."

"Just talk with Nadine. Tell me if I've been wrong."

Randall snorted. "Can't you see that's what she wants? To confuse you? To work on your sympathies till you relinquish your plan to send her to Ireland?"

"The young cock has a point, Johnny," admitted Lord Peter. "There is a chance she may be trying to create a reasonable doubt in your mind, so you'll—"

"Take her off the hook?" interrupted John with the ghost of a smile.

"That's very good! Where did you pick it up?" asked Randall, struck by the phrase.

"From my wife. She says it's common usage in the twentieth century. She has a number of interesting turns of speech."

Lord Peter rested his hand briefly on his friend's

shoulder. "Tomorrow at two."

"Thank you. And you, Randy? Will you accompany our Peter to make sure his soft heart doesn't betray his sober judgment?"

"Soft head is more like it," grumbled Randall, rising and pulling the bell-rope for his servant. "We're off to Tattersall's to look at the horseflesh. Will you join us?"

"No, I've one more call to make. There is someone who may know a great deal about this situation—"

"Another doctor, John?" interrupted Randall. "Do you go to secure a second medical opinion?"

"No, I'm going to the House of Parliament. There's a man there who may have some answers. Edmund Burke. He's political secretary to Lord Rockingham. If anyone knows about the situation in America, Burke does."

After Lord John had taken his leave, the two friends regarded one another gloomily.

"Parliament!" Randall sighed in exasperation. "It's my belief Johnny's touched in his loft."

"Poor Johnny."

"That cursed female!" Randall said bitterly. "She's made his life a hell. He hasn't been his own man since he married her. Damme, it's like witchcraft!"

"Being Johnny, he has to give her every chance," said Lord Peter. "What d'you suppose she's up to now?"

"She's wicked, Peter. She even cast out lures to me— her husband's best friend! I told her I'd as soon embrace a cobra. She hasn't spoken to me since."

Peter was forced to smile. "You're a little diplomat, aren't you?"

"You know what she is! How can we help her to ruin Johnny's life?"

"And who," said Lord Peter lazily, "says we are going to help her?"

Five

At *exactly* two o'clock on the following day, there was a discreet rap on milady's bedroom door. Bennet rose from the chair where she had been reading her Bible and went quietly to open the door, trying not to waken the woman who was asleep on the great bed.

A footman whispered importantly, "Lord Peter Masterson, Mr. Randall Towne, present their compliments to her ladyship. Beg to wait upon her."

Bennet's first impulse was to deny the intrusion. Then she recalled that these gentlemen were his lordship's closest friends, and as such might feel it incumbent upon them to inquire after Lady Elsingham. And there had been pitifully few sympathy calls. Her beautiful charge had no friends in London. A kindly gesture might encourage her, lift her from the depression into which she seemed to have sunk. So, finger to lip, she considered the situation. After a moment she replied, "I shall see if her ladyship is awake."

When she reached the bedside, her charge was regarding her through eyes wide with alarm.

"Oh, what is happening, Bennet? Is it more trouble?"

Bennet's soft heart was wrung with pity. "No, no, milady, 'tis only two good friends of his lordship's, come to pay their respects. Are you well enough to receive them?"

Kathryn sighed with relief. "Lord John's friends? Of course I'll see them. Who are they, Bennet? Do I—know them well?"

As she raised the beautiful shoulders, plumped up pillows, straightened the covers and smoothed back the glorious hair, Bennet was worriedly considering that very problem. Strange and terrible as milady's story was, Bennet had become a believer. She had encountered nothing remotely like this situation in all her quiet, God-fearing life. Considered sensibly, the story was impossible. Worse, it smacked of witchcraft and the forbidden arts. But Bennet had looked deep into the strange green eyes, and listened to the tortured voice, and something inside her accepted the fact that this woman believed she was telling the exact truth. Bennet hadn't got any further than that. She prayed every night, and served her charge every day, exactly as she had loved and served and prayed for Lord John when he had been a small boy and her special responsibility.

She answered Kathryn's question. "Yes, you know them. But it is said in the servant's hall that you don't like them very much."

"Oh, dear! How do I address them, Bennet?"

Bennet surprised herself. "Milady, I think you

should begin as you mean to go on. If you intend to maintain your story, you must be—yourself."

This startled a small laugh from Kathryn. "No compromise! *Full speed ahead and damn the torpedoes!* That's a quotation from Admiral Farragut, and it's good American, Bennet. Bless you!"

"Full speed ahead," acknowledged Bennet, confused but loyal, "and—er—damn the torpedoes!" She returned to the door, and flinging it open with quite a fine flourish, told the startled footman, "Her ladyship will see the gentlemen."

What Kathryn saw as the visitors entered her bedroom was, first, an enormous bunch of flowers carried by a man even taller than Lord John and reassuringly pleasant of countenance. His attitude as he advanced toward her was easy and open. And then she saw that the eyes, a hard dark gray, were scrutinizing her face intently. She turned to look at the other man with a sense of escape.

The second man was younger, dark, almost sullen-looking. He seemed to be avoiding her glance. Instead he addressed himself to Bennet. "What ho, Mistress Bennet! It is good to see you again!"

Kathryn turned to the big man, who was proffering his flowers. He laid them gently on the coverlet. "My lady. I hope we see you much improved," he said, formally.

"Yes, indeed, sir. Dr. Anders tells me that my arm is knitting nicely. I was a little apprehensive, since your doctors haven't discovered antibiotics yet, but Dr. Anders seems both kind and competent in the medical knowledge of this century."

Even Bennet looked startled. This was carrying the war into the enemy camp with a vengeance. Kathryn felt a stir of pure pleasure at the dangerous game she had decided to play. Be yourself, Bennet had advised. Well, Kathryn Hendrix of the twentieth century would do it!

The big man was frowning slightly. "Anti—what was that, milady?"

"Antibiotics. Chemical substances which inhibit the growth of bacteria. Or have your doctors discovered the existence of bacteria yet? I can't recall. After all, I was a history minor at my college, not a pre-med student."

Avoiding Bennet's cautioning glance, Kathryn looked instead at Lord John's friends with as keen a scrutiny as they were directing at her. The slighter youth had dropped his jaw in a reflex of astonishment. The bigger man had his lazy eyes fully open now, and they were puzzled rather than hard. Kathryn decided rashly to pursue the attack before they could recover and re-group. She'd show these arrogant Englishmen!

"I'm told you are the two best friends Lord John has, so I would like to be civil to you. I don't know which of you is which. Would you be gracious enough to introduce yourselves? I am Kathryn Hendrix of New York, very unwilling to be here in this rather fulsome body, and disturbed by the situation Lady Nadine seems to have gotten herself into. Since," she concluded with a wry smile, "I seem to have inherited the unpleasant results of it."

Lord Peter saluted her with a smile of reluctant admiration. "No quarter, ma'am? You are determined to maintain your position, however—untenable?"

"As I have just told Bennet, my course must be full speed ahead, and damn the torpedoes! Which is a quotation from one of our American admirals in a civil war fought between the Northern and Southern United States starting in 1861."

"I salute your courage, ma'am, but beg to offer you

a warning," replied Lord Peter quietly. "The story you are telling is incredible. Have you carefully considered the consequences of persisting in such—"

"Such a preposterous lie!" interrupted Randall hotly. "I'll give you the truth with the bark on it, madam. Whatever devious game you're playing, you can't win. No one can win. The kindest judgment will be that you are mad—the worst, that you are dabbling in witchcraft!"

Kathryn stared at the flushed, angry face of the young man. "If the cry of witchcraft is raised, I would have you consider that I have been the victim of it, not the instigator. I am snatched from my own time and place and brought to this—" she glanced at Peter and checked what she was going to say, substituting, "this very inhospitable situation, locked into the body of a woman for whom no one can have anything but contempt. You are Lord John's friends. What would you advise me to do?"

"Have done with playacting and go back to Ireland," snapped Randall. "You're nothing but trouble here."

Kathryn turned to Lord Peter with a faint smile. "And you, my lord? Do you subscribe to this severe judgment?"

"Severe, madam?" Randall interjected. "'Tis the soul of leniency! After what you've done to Johnny—"

"What *I've* done—!" began Kathryn in protest, then, facing Randall's scornful expression, she sighed and turned to his companion.

"There are reasons why it would be very hazardous—perhaps disastrous—for me to leave London at this moment," she began, aware of the hardening of suspicion on Lord Peter's face. "I need to remain as close as possible to the place through which I entered your world—"

"Faugh!" interrupted Randall. "More of your mystical nonsense! I don't know why we listen to you!"

"You actually haven't, have you? Not really." She sighed. "I was taught to be properly appreciative of gifts. And so, Lord Peter or Mr. Towne, whichever you are," she smiled wanly at the big, serious Lord Peter, "thank you very much for the beautiful flowers. And to you," she turned to the angry Randall, "my thanks for your honesty. I understand my position more clearly now. Good day."

It was dismissal. The gentlemen made their bows and got out of the room with what grace they could muster. Randall was fuming.

"Trickster! Liar! Cheat!" he muttered, as they went down the great stairway. "When I think of Johnny tied to that Irish termagant—!"

When his friend did not respond at once, Randy eyed him sharply. "Don't tell me she's pulled the wool over your eyes?"

Lord Peter shook his head. "I think the honors go to her. We didn't really listen, did we? We had our minds made up before we came."

Randall spat out an oath. "How much do I need to know? I tell you the woman tried to seduce me! Not two months ago! 'Whoever you are,' says she, like Mistress Prim and Proper. I'm Johnny's best friend. She knew it then and she knows it now!"

Lord Peter shook his head. "Whatever the case, the sooner Johnny ships her off to Ireland, the better things will be for both of them."

Six

When the gentleman had left, Bennet closed the door behind them gently. Her face wore a worried look. Kathryn smiled ruefully at her.

"Tell me, Bennet. Go on! I didn't handle that very well, did I?"

"Oh, my lady, they're very powerful men, for all the young one seems like such a boy. And they're his lordship's best friends."

Kathryn shrugged wearily. Her arm was throbbing with the dull pain that never stopped, her head ached, perhaps as a result of the emotional tension she had just experienced. She drew a deep breath, raggedly. "I guess I'm a fool, Bennet. But they *didn't* listen! No one does."

Bennet's warm heart was pierced by the look of desolation on the beautiful face. The strange pale green eyes were smudged around with dark shadows, the exquisite mouth drooped at the corners. She went over to the bed and patted the invalid's silken shoulder gently.

"I'll listen, milady. What can I do to help you?"

"You mean that?"

"You know I do," the older woman said stoutly.

"Yes, I do know. And I thank God for you. One thing you could do that would help me more than I can say, would be for you to call me by my name."

"Your name, milady?" faltered Bennet.

"Kathryn. Just to show that one person in all this horrible world doesn't believe I am insane!" Kathryn ended with a sob.

Bennet patted her shoulder again, more firmly. "Of course you're not insane, Miss Kathryn," she said sternly. "What sort of foolish talk is that?"

Kathryn looked up at her with a reluctant smile pulling at her lips. "Oh, Bennet, you fraud! You remind me of a story in the Bible. No, I'm not being sacrilegious," she answered the startled look on Bennet's face. "It's the story of the father of the epileptic in Caesarea Philippi: 'I believe, O Lord; help Thou my unbelief!'"

Bennet faced Kathryn with a new light in her eyes. "Miss Kathryn, I *believe* you. Now, d'ye ken how we're going to solve your problem?" and the warm Scots' burr was strong in her voice.

Sudden tears of gratitude flooded Kathryn's eyes. She brushed them away and said quickly, "I have been thinking about that every moment today. It seems to me that if I... *came here* because of that portrait, maybe that's my way back."

Bennet nodded doubtfully. "That would seem to

make sense, but how would you go about it? Had you thought of that?"

"Well, I could try to recreate the conditions as closely as I could to what they were when I—came. It was during a storm in New York. I was staring at the portrait and a bright light above it was almost dazzling my eyes..."

"We could get you down to the landing to stand in front of the portrait, and I could arrange for enough candles above it on the gallery to make' the bright light—but your arm..." Bennet frowned. "The lower hallway would be full of servants at that hour. There might even be guests of his lordship—"

Kathryn shook her head. "That won't do. I'd have to have complete quiet. And there's another thing," she added hesitantly. "If there *was* any kind of trickery— or witchcraft—involved..." She caught the look of alarm on Bennet's face. "How do I know what caused me to come, what brought me here? It seemed to me that the beautiful eyes of the portrait were alive... and evil... and that they were drawing me... into the picture... pulling me—"

"God save us!" whispered Bennet, wide-eyed.

"I guess I've lost you, Bennet."

"That you haven't, Miss Kathryn, you poor lamb, and let me hear no more of such 'cavey talk! I'm just recalling gossip in the servants' hall when that creature Donner wasn't about. Everyone thinks she's in league with the Devil. She's that cold and mysterious and ugly, and always muttering about what will happen to those that cross her..." Bennet suppressed a shudder. "I could believe anything of·her, Miss Kathryn, I could indeed."

They were interrupted by a tap on the door, which

immediately opened. Lord John stood on the threshold, and behind him waited Dr. Anders and a slender, ugly man very plainly dressed.

"May we come in?" asked Lord John, doing so without waiting for permission.

Kathryn felt the thrust of emotion which this arrogant Englishman seemed always able to arouse in her.

"Please do," she managed to say coolly. "Dr. Anders, I'm glad to see you. My arm is aching so intolerably I'm sure it must be healing nicely."

Dr. Anders sketched a bow. "It is good to see you in spirits, milady," he said cautiously, advancing to the bedside.

"Do I have a fever, doctor? I'm sure you have Mr. Fahrenheit's thermometer, since he invented it early in this century. But no antibiotics! Medicine is handicapped in this age. How long ago was it that the only recourse for a broken limb was amputation? At least we must be thankful that skillful practitioners are not the exclusive property of any period in history, for you've set and splinted my arm most successfully. Are you a student of Dr. Potts?"

Dr. Anders peered at her sharply. "I am aware of Dr. Percival Potts' fine treatise on the subject of Fractures and Dislocations, milady, but it surprises me a little that you should know of it. It is true, as her ladyship says," and he directed his speech to the other two men, "that even as short a period as twenty years ago, physicians were recommending amputation for compound fractures. Your own fracture, however, was a simple one, Lady Nadine."

"That should serve to depress my pretensions," said Kathryn, with a demure glance at the gentlemen.

A smile touched Lord John's lips involuntarily. She

was spirited, this Irish wife of his! And her wits were as sharp as his own. It was absurd to consider her mad. But if not insanity, what? Artifice? She was fighting for something, with this strange tale of hers—her desire to be accepted as someone other than Nadine. Could she be fighting for—him? Surely not to win him back? She had shown, with humiliating insistence, just what she thought of her lord and master. But even as he cringed at certain memories, a small glow of excitement began to burn in his body. Was this beautiful creature fighting to win him back? He scanned the lovely face. Was it changed? Was there a new sweetness about the set of the lips, a new, more honest light in those fascinating, pale green eyes?

He caught himself short, setting his jaw. Fool! Double damned fool. This was the very trap he had fallen into a year ago in Ireland, the day he met the young Irish beauty riding her great roan horse through the deep green meadows and through the dark copses. He had fallen in love with an ideal—a woman who wasn't there. *Enough of these adolescent idiocies,* Lord John told himself sternly. *You know what she is. Only a fool would let himself be caught twice in the same trap.*

He turned to introduce the stranger, who had had no eyes for anything else in the exquisitely-furnished room after he had caught one glimpse of the woman in the bed.

"My lady, may I present Mr. Wilmot Manton? He is an associate of a brilliant countryman of yours, Edmund Burke. And he's very eager indeed to hear what you can tell him of the state of affairs in the Colonies."

Kathryn stared into Lord John's cold eyes. Was he taunting her or offering her a chance to prove her claim? There was nothing to be read from his narrow, social smile.

"I am very happy to meet you, Mr. Manton," she said, smiling up into his admiring face. "I'm sure you've heard about the Boston Tea Party, since it occurred on December 16, 1773, but there might be later events which I could discuss. Lord Elsingham may have told you that I have sources of information not available to the average person living in London in this Year of Grace 1775."

There! That was carrying the battle into the enemy's camp with a vengeance! She thought she caught an expression of admiration lurking on Lord John's handsome face, but she was committed to the fight now, and could not indulge her heart with weakening emotions. She drew a careful breath.

"It would help me very much if you could give me the exact date, Mr. Manton."

Manton, already a little wary at this lovely lady's hint that she had information not available to legitimate offices in His Majesty's service, was jerked rudely from his earlier admiration by this odd question. "The date, milady? But why—what . . . ?"

Help came to Kathryn from an unexpected source.

"Why, ma'am," said Lord John smoothly, "you've been suffering with your broken arm for several days. It is scarcely to be wondered at if you have lost count of the time. This is the eighteenth of April, in the year of Our Lord 1775."

Kathryn flashed him a smile of such sweetness that his heart jolted treacherously. "I thank you, milord," she said, and turned again to Mr. Manton.

"Tomorrow, that is April nineteenth, General Gage will send soldiers to capture or destroy military stores at Concord. The mission will be unsuccessful because the colonists will have advance knowledge of the attack and will meet and counter it with the first armed resistance to British troops at Lexington Green..."

Alarm and disbelief battled for supremacy on Manton's face. "This is not military intelligence, ma'am," he spluttered. "This is prophecy! How came you by this knowledge?"

Kathryn paled. Fool! By her desire to prove herself knowledgeable she had probably doomed herself to incarceration in Bedlam. Dr. Anders was frowning heavily. Her eyes met Lord John's. Was there pity, concern for her, in their gray depths? She went on grimly, "If you will jot it down, Mr. Manton, and a few other things I have to tell you, then when the time comes, we shall see whether I have informed you correctly."

Manton was staring from Kathryn to Lord John, unable to decide whether this was some aristocratic hoax or a stupid attempt to entrap Burke and Burke's sponsor, Lord Rockingham. His self-esteem wounded, he said stiffly, "If there should be any such attack, it would take from three to four weeks for the intelligence to reach us. Whatever my opinion of General Gage's orders, I still respect the laws of time and space. It is impossible that her ladyship could have such knowledge. If you will excuse me, milord, I shall return at once to the House, where I have duties." He sketched a bow toward Kathryn and left the room.

Kathryn held out her free arm, palm up in a gesture which at once confessed frustration and offered apology.

"I wasn't very convincing, was I?"

Lord John turned to face the little doctor. "Anders, can you possibly believe that Lady Nadine's mind and speech are those of a Bedlamite? She is in perfect possession of her senses. She is as clearheaded as either of us!"

Dr. Anders brooded a moment, frowning at Kathryn.

"Well, milord," he said grudgingly, "you'd better convince her ladyship to stop playing this game, or we'll be compelled to commit her." He gave a reluctant chuckle. "The look on that prissy fellow's mug was worth the price of admission."

He turned to Kathryn. "I don't know what you're up to, ma'am, but I'd better warn you it's a chancy business. Be advised by your husband, and leave off these maneuvers. 'Tis a losing game, milady. You'll get no good of it, and maybe more grief than you can handle."

The doctor took his leave. With a worried, challenging look at Kathryn, Lord John went out after him.

"Bennet!" cried Kathryn as the door closed. "Slip out after them and see if you can hear what Dr. Anders says to Lord John. I don't like all that advice Anders was giving me. It had a sort of 'final warning' tone to it."

Bennet obeyed hastily. Kathryn sat up in bed, cradling her splinted forearm till the little woman returned. The expression on Bennet's face sent a chill through the younger woman's body.

"You were right, Miss Kathryn," whispered Bennet. "What Dr. Anders was saying sounded like a final warning. He said, 'You had better convince her ladyship to drop this masquerade or whatever farradiddle she thinks she is playing at. Manton will have it all over town that she's insane or in league with the powers of darkness.'

"'No one would believe such an absurdity,' his lordship came back at him.

"'Would they not? You know polite society better than I do, milord, but even I know that such a rumor could ruin not only your lady wife but yourself. And I might remind you that a woman was burned as a witch in Scotland as late as 1727,' the doctor rattles

72

back at his lordship," Bennet was whispering when the door opened abruptly and Lord John came in. His face was set.

"Well, Nadine, have I given you enough proof that this latest stratagem of yours is unworkable? You are getting yourself in deeper waters than you dream of. In God's name, for your own sake if not for any feeling you might have for me, drop this most dangerous game!" He glanced at Bennet. "Perhaps you can convince Lady Nadine that she has embarked upon a disastrous course. If not, I shall have to send her off to Ireland tomorrow—for her own protection."

He left the room.

Behind him there was the frozen silence of despair.

Seven

While *Kathryn* and Bennet stared at one another, there came a tap on the door. Bennet stumbled over to see what new threat was arriving. A footman stolidly presented a rather grimy note, carefully sealed and superscribed *for Lady Nadine Elsingham.*

"Just delivered by hand," the footman advised.

Bennet dismissed him and brought the note to Kathryn.

"Open it for me, Bennet. I'm so awkward with this arm," fretted Kathryn.

The note was short:

My lady—Donner has arranged passige home for her nursling on the Irish Mail packet from Liverpool. Ther will be a privat kerrige waiting at the

Black Swan at 10 tomoro morning. Ile be in it, waiting an reddy to look ater you an get you safly home to the dere contry.

Bring all yer jools and whatever monny you can lay hands on. I have yer nightime potion by me, so you can rest like you were wont before that Englishman seporated us.

Then, in a more literate hand, was scrawled,

Beware, Nadine! The Englishman is going to have you confined in Bedlam. The word of it is all over London.

Donner's crabbed signature closed the letter.

"Well," said Kathryn grimly, "I have no choice. Stay here and be sent to Bedlam, wait and be sent to Ireland at my lord's whim, or go to Ireland tomorrow with Donner."

"You'd never do that last, Miss Kathryn!" protested Bennet. "See, the shameless creature is coaxing you with promises of that drug she was in the habit of giving you—"

Kathryn interrupted her. "Donner is the last person I'd go anywhere with," she reassured Bennet. "Every time she came near me I felt an actual sickness. She's the witch, Bennet. But what's this about a drug?"

"Remember the little brown bottle she tried to dose you with that night you fell? Dr. Anders had the contents tested. He told Lord John it was a—mind-destroying drug," Bennet reported. "Dr. Anders said you should probably be under constant supervision, for your own sake, lest worse symptoms develop, and Lord John was swearing he'd have Donner sent to prison."

Kathryn thought hard. "Bennet," she said slowly, "it seems to me there is only one thing I can do. I've got to try to get back to my own time and place, the only way I know how..."

Bennet, frightened but resolute, said, "You mean—through the portrait?"

Kathryn nodded. "It seems crazy... but I did get here that way, no matter what anyone says. So I've got to try to get back the same way."

"Shall we try now?"

Kathryn gave her a grateful smile. "It's too early. Too many people around, to see me and try to stop me. But you can get a supply of candles to make the light we talked about. Perhaps I was hypnotized by it, or something. I think it's part of—the way."

Bennet was chilled by a sudden thought she didn't dare to voice. What if the drug—that devil's potion Donner had been giving this poor child—was also 'part of the way'? She clasped her hands in agonized indecision. Mind-destroying? Essential?

Kathryn was speaking. "As soon as the household settles down, I'll go to the main hallway and stand in front of the picture. I'd better wear that awful golden-orange dress Nadine was wearing—I'm sure that I *must* have everything the same as it was that night. Can you find the dress for me, Bennet?"

"I'm sure I can, Miss Kathryn," Bennet assured her. "I'll go right away and get candles and look for the dress." She was glad to be doing anything to get her mind off the horrifying thought that the experiment would never succeed without some of the drug from the brown bottle. Was there any way she could get some? She didn't even know what it was, or how much to administer. Too much might kill the child. Oh, dear! this was a frightening business! As she trudged down the servants' stairway at the rear of the great London mansion, her thoughts scurried hither and yon. She felt like a small terrier determined to overcome a very large and menacing wolf pack.

She had no trouble in getting a large number of candles up to her room. No one on the staff would think of questioning Lady Nadine's personal maid, even if Bennet had not been long and favorably known to most of them as one who knew and kept her rightful place. As his lordship's old nurse, she was equal in standing to the butler, Mr. Burl, himself.

She had little more difficulty in finding her ladyship's gown. It had already been neatly mended and cleaned, and was hanging in the sewing room waiting to be restored to her ladyship's extensive wardrobe. Still Bennet was not satisfied. Putting on her neat dark shawl and bonnet, she delegated one of the upstair maids to listen for her ladyship's bell while she ran an errand in town. For Bennet, gentle soul and devoted servant, had conceived a daring plan. She would go to Dr. Anders' consulting rooms and try to get the brown bottle.

Fortune favored her scheme. The doctor was out on a call, but his manservant recognized Bennet as the trusted Elsingham servant who had first brought the bottle to the doctor. He accepted, after some demur, the request, purported to come from his lordship himself, that the bottle be returned for some unspecified purpose. Bennet carried it off with a fine air of authority, but had the doctor's servant not been already totally convinced of the fact that the "Quality" were all unreasonable and completely irrational in their demands, she might have had a harder time. As it was, the man shrugged and found the bottle for her in his master's desk.

Bennet hastened back to the Elsingham town house. She went at once to Kathryn's room and confessed what she had done and why. Kathryn was delighted at her wisdom and enterprise.

"I'd never have thought of it," she marveled, "but of course, the drug is essential. It must be!"

Bennet was already having second thoughts. She almost wished she hadn't thought of it. "What if we give you too much?" she fretted. "There's neither of us knows aught about the dosage—and Dr. Anders as much as said the stuff was deadly! Mind-destroying, he called it!"

"Well, my mind's not destroyed, whatever happened to Lady Nadine's," Kathryn replied firmly. "Bennet, don't weaken now. You've been a tower of strength and a friend in need and I do not know what I would have done without you. I'd better eat something and then rest until you come to help me dress—after everyone is asleep, Bennet," she added.

Bennet nodded and went to order a particularly nourishing meal for the intrepid time traveler. Bennet was wishing she could confide in her nursling, now grown to such a tall and splendid man—but with, alas, a will of his own and an inflexible desire to have his commands obeyed.

Kathryn too was having second thoughts. It had suddenly struck her that she was having the most exciting time of her hitherto colorless life. She got up and, slightly staggering after her days in bed, went toward the largest of the many mirrors with which the room was liberally supplied. Standing in the bright light of the candles which flanked it, she had a sudden surge of delight as she met the eyes of the lovely creature in the glass.

"Ravishing," she said with a chuckle. "My girl, you

may have been a tartar and a termagant, but you certainly are a knock-out. Pity you didn't have more sense than to let yourself be manipulated by that weirdo Donner. Because as Lady Nadine Elsingham, baby, you really had it made."

"Why do you say that?" came a deep voice behind her.

Kathryn whirled, panic-stricken. Lord John was standing in the doorway. "How did you get in—" she began, and then blushed. He was Nadine's husband. It was his right—

Lord John came into the room and shut the door behind him. He advanced toward her, watching her with interest. "I don't believe I've ever seen you blush before. It is most becoming."

Kathryn, blushing harder, could find nothing to say.

Lord John came a step closer. "Do you know . . . I find myself nearer to believing this story of yours than ever before? It isn't so much the things you were saying as you looked into the glass. It was the way you said them. You truly believe that you are someone else, don't you? I hadn't accepted that before."

"My lord," said Kathryn soberly, "as God is my witness, I am Kathryn Hendrix of New York—to the best of my knowledge and belief."

The big man looked at her, his eyes less cold than she had ever seen them. "Yes, you believe it. So what are we to do, Kathryn-Nadine—whoever you think you are? Have you a solution for our problem? Do you want to stay here—with me?"

An involuntary shiver of delight went through Kathryn at the sound of that deep male voice. And he noticed it—and in his eyes there leaped a fire such as Kathryn had never seen in a man's gaze before. She drew back from the force of it, just as Lord John took the last step which brought them face to face.

"I am without doubt the greatest fool God ever made, but I'm going to ask you. In spite of everything that has happened between us—in spite of the folly and the quarreling and the shame—shall we try again, Nadine?" His voice was low and husky with passion, and something in Kathryn responded to it with an intensity she had never known in all her lonely life. Almost without willing it, she was in his arms, strong arms that yet, even in that moment of passionate attraction, remembered to hold her injured arm gently, protectively . . .

While their lips still clung and her mind refused to function, Kathryn felt deep within some inner small core of commonsense crying out that this ecstasy was not for her. She told herself that it was the beautiful body of Nadine that this man loved, not the mind and soul of Kathryn Hendrix. Could she remain in this place and time, aware always that she was a substitute—aware always that not only Lord John but everyone who knew them would remember the ugly things Nadine had done? A vision of the contempt in Randall's eyes and the stern judgment in Lord Peter's face flashed into her mind, and she drew herself out of Lord John's embrace.

"No!"

It was no more than a breath of rejection, but he heard it. Almost reluctantly he pulled himself away from her. He loomed above her, a big blond giant of a man, staring down intently into her face. Had Kathryn been less distracted, she would have been aware of the wakening trust in the man's eyes, the almost desperate desire to believe in her—or to believe that this beautiful, wanton child had matured into the woman he had dreamed of when first he saw her, breath-taking in her dark green habit, the glorious auburn hair flying in the wind as she rode her powerful hunter across the green field. But Kathryn was too full of her plans for return to her own time to be sensitive to the man's reactions. She had not considered the ultimate hazard this place might offer—that she might feel tenderness—*face it!*—might even fall in love with a man who had died a hundred years before her own birth. It was impossible! She drew away, trembling, and Lord John, a mature and sophisticated man, recognized at once the difference between this trembling and the shiver of desire his wife had felt a moment before. Still, there was the new and exciting look in those fascinating green eyes, a look they had never held for him before. He frowned.

"What is it? What troubles you so? I am willing to come half way—to forgive and forget—to begin again with what we have. You cannot deny that we do have ... something for each other?"

At that moment Kathryn knew that she had fallen under the spell of this virile man. Beside him, poor Don faded to a miserable creature, a conniver, an opportunist. She realized with gratitude that she would never grieve for Donald Madson again. Better nothing than that pallid excuse for love she had felt. But this man posed a real threat. He was dangerously attractive, disturbing to her peace of mind. If she yielded to his charm now, she would be frozen here forever in this body, in the persona of a woman for whom no one could have respect—not even Lord John. Not even herself. On his terms: to be Nadine, the forgiven sinner, always to be watched lest the old trouble recur.

Intolerable.

Kathryn drew back a step or two. "My lord," she began, and her voice trembled in spite of her effort to control it.

Lord John smiled a little, tenderly. Kathryn noted that it was a singularly attractive smile. "Call me by my name, Na-Kathryn," he suggested. "As you did in Paris."

But the damage had been done. "Na-Kathryn." That's what she would be, if she weakened and let herself stay here. An afterthought, the weak echo of another woman.

"John," she complied, fighting desperately to avoid his gaze, his warmth, his exciting presence. "Will you permit me to rest now? I'm still pretty shaky. We can...continue our discussion tomorrow, when I am rested and calmer."

Lord John accepted his dismissal with perfect courtesy. "Of course, my dear. Although I for one do not anticipate that you and I will ever be able to discuss this issue calmly." His smile was rueful as he bowed and went quietly from the room.

Watching his broad shoulders in the faultlessly tailored coat, Kathryn knew that her heart would betray her if she had to have any more 'discussions' with this nobleman.

Entering an hour later, Bennet found Kathryn seated in an armchair near the dying fire. Bennet was carrying the golden dress. "Miss Kathryn," she whispered, "everyone's gone to bed. I've lighted the candles—there's a proper blaze above the portrait. Lady Nadine had new sconces installed, just so her picture would be well-lighted for the reception. She was a very vain young woman," finished the older woman with a disapproving shake of the head.

Kathryn smiled ruefully. "Well, we'll have to admit that she had plenty to be vain about," she commented. Bennet didn't know whether to be shocked or amused, considering the lips from which the words were coming, but she joined Kathryn's soft laughter.

"I can't seem to connect you with her," she whispered. "Not that I was that close to Lady Nadine. Donner held everyone at arm's length; keeping the poor child under control, I suppose. But it was impossible to mistake her character—"

"And mine is different?" invited Kathryn.

But Bennet wouldn't be led into flattery. "Come now, Miss Kathryn, we've got to get you into this garish bit of a costume and down to the landing before someone wakes and discovers what we're about." She hesitated. "Are you sure, Miss Kathryn? Very sure that this is the only way?"

"I'm sure, Bennet. Don't confuse me."

"Never," vowed Bennet devoutly, and assisted Kathryn into the dress.

"I don't think it'll matter if my hair isn't fixed exactly the same," whispered Kathryn. "Anyway, I could never get it to look that way again. It must have taken an hour."

"An hour?" sniffed Bennet. "More like three or four! And looked a proper rats' nest at the end of it!"

In spite of—or perhaps because of—the serious nature of their project, the two women found themselves giggling wildly over a joke that really wasn't funny. "We're getting hysterical," cautioned Kathryn. "We'd better go down to the landing quickly, before I lose my nerve."

"That reminds me," whispered Bennet as they left the exquisite room for the last time—Kathryn hoped— "I've got this," and she held out the little bottle.

Kathryn drew in her breath sharply. "Bennet! Do you think we should? How much of it should I take?"

They were in front of the portrait now, very conscious of the mocking light in those painted, sea-green eyes that stared so insolently down at them.

"I don't know, milady," confessed Bennet, forgetting the 'Miss Kathryn' in her distress of spirit. "I'm not even sure you should take any of it—but there's little doubt, if what that creature said was true, that Lady Nadine was full of it, the night—the night you changed places."

"Do you know," said Kathryn with an air of discovery, "I've never for one moment thought of *her*—of Lady Nadine. If I came here, did she go to the picture gallery in New York? I wonder what she thought of plain Miss Hendrix's body—and that awful old coat?" She began to giggle compulsively. Bennet shushed her quickly.

"Miss Kathryn! You'll have them all down on us! Tell me, what must I do?"

"Well, you'd better give me a few drops of that drug— I'll try first with a little—"

"You will try no such thing in my house," came a voice of such icy contempt that Kathryn felt her flesh shrink. "I should have known not to expect truth or decency from you, Nadine. But to have drawn poor innocent Bennet into your filthy schemes— Give me that!" and Lord John, white with rage, snatched the small bottle from Kathryn's nerveless fingers. He towered over the two trembling women, his anger so plainly written on his face that neither of them dared offer any excuse.

"You will go to your room at once, madam, and I shall lock you in it. As for you, Bennet, it would be better for you to stay in your room until Lady Nadine and I have left for Liverpool in the morning. Send one of the maids to pack for milady. I'm sorry you should have been drawn into this imbroglio."

He stood in the blaze of light from the candles, obviously controlling his anger with difficulty, looking, thought Kathryn miserably, like Judgment Day. Hating herself for her meekness, Kathryn crept upstairs to the room she had hoped never to enter again. She was scarcely inside when she heard the key turn in the lock. Dragging herself to the bed, she lay down, too despairing even to weep.

Eight

Kathryn lay on the bed for a long time, staring straight above her. Her thoughts went in despairing circles; it seemed impossible to control them. Her eyes ached with the effort of holding them open. She noticed for the first time that the ceiling of the tester bed was exquisitely painted—a lounging Venus, red-haired, was surrounded by a bevy of little cupids. Kathryn hated the silly sensuality of the painting, though in a happier hour she might have found it charming.

But now there was only chagrin, frustration, fear of what was to happen to her in this alien time and place. She had so little control over events! It seemed she could be exiled from the one place where she might have any chance of undoing whatever had happened to her, sent away by a man's arrogant, unreasonable whim . . .

What would happen to her in Ireland?

At last the unwelcome thought intruded that she might indeed be the crazy creature Lord John obviously thought her. And there was no one to believe—to help...

Into the depths of her anguish intruded a gentle scratching sound, very persistent. Kathryn lowered her gaze from the exquisitely painted ceiling to search out the source of the noise. It was coming from the region of the door. After a moment the door swung silently open and a small figure slipped inside, closed the door quietly, and locked it again.

"Oh, Bennet!" wailed Kathryn, and the tears came in a healing flood.

"Hush, now, child," cautioned Bennet, her own eyes very bright in the candlelight. "No one must know I am here."

"Will we try to get through the portrait again?" asked Kathryn humbly. "I'm not sure I'm up to it, after what's happened."

"'Twould be no use, Miss Kathryn," said Bennet bitterly. "His lordship's had the painting taken down. Roused one of the footmen to help him. I've never seen him so angry." She sighed. "He was a sunny little lad."

"Then that is the end of it," Kathryn's voice was dead. "I'll be sent to Ireland in the morning. Thank you, Bennet, for being my friend."

Bennet lifted one finger admonishingly. "No more of that, Miss Kathryn," she said, as though the younger woman were a child and she the nurse. "It is not like you to give in to defeat. I've come to help you. What shall we do next?"

Bennet's plump face was stern with purpose. Kathryn opened her eyes wider. This was support indeed! She would have to prove herself worthy of this intrepid partisan. She began to feel better. Later, there would be time to relive that dreadful moment when Lord John's eyes had passed over her with such icy contempt—the eyes she knew could warm to passionate intensity. *But never again for me,* she thought. Nadine—and I, too—have finally killed even the tiny spark of faith he had left.

"Miss Kathryn, I have an idea," Bennet was saying quietly. "You'll dress in some of my clothes, with a cape to hide your bandaged arm. You'll leave the house with me before dawn. We'll go to the posting house from which the coaches take off for the north, and we'll get you a ticket for Elsinghurst Village. That's the village that serves the Manor, his lordship's country estate," she explained. "I'll give you a letter to my brother Richard. We have a farm several miles outside the village. Lord John's father gave it to my brother and me when Lord John left for school and I was no longer needed as his nurse. Well, you'll arrive at Elsinghurst about dusk, when everybody's indoors, eating. Just walk back down the road the way the coach has been coming—" she paused, noting the pale strained face with which Kathryn had been following her instructions.

"No, no, my dearie! What's wrong with me? You'll no' be able to walk several miles after that long, weary ride, and you not well at all!"

"Your plan is better than Lord John's," Kathryn said quietly. "Perhaps I might stop at the inn at Elsinghurst, and ask the landlord to send someone for your brother."

"That'd be a sure way to inform every gossip in the country that a beautiful stranger had arrived in the village. From that, it'd be no more than a cat's blink till everyone knew that the Lady of Elsingham was at the inn. Och! and I was sure I had such a famous idea!"

It was Kathryn's turn to rally her companion's failing spirits. "It is an excellent idea! It just needs a little adjusting. Now, let's see: Is there any other way to get to the farm than through Elsinghurst Village?"

Bennet nodded eagerly. "Twenty miles before you come to Elsinghurst, there's a place called Crofton. It's larger than Elsinghurst, and has two inns. You could dismount from the coach there, and take a room at the smaller of the two inns. Send a boy with my letter to Richard, and stay inside the room until Richard comes for you." Bennet nodded decisively. "That will serve! Our farm's about half way between Crofton and Elsinghurst. Richard could get to one place as well as the other. And he'll be proud to keep you safe until we can work out something better."

The enormity of what she was asking a completely unknown man to do suddenly became plain to Kathryn. "I can't!" she objected. "Think, Bennet! A strange woman dropping in on him from nowhere! He'll hate it."

"Not Richard," said Bennet proudly. "Though I say it myself, as shouldn't, Richard Bennet is the kindest man in all of England. And Scotland, too," she added, after a second's thought.

Kathryn considered rapidly. The night was passing, and she must make some decision before dawn if she hoped to escape the exile to Ireland, where the frightening Donner might have to be dealt with. There were objections to Bennet's scheme—too many to list—but it might work, if she were lucky, and if Richard Bennet would accept the responsibility.

"There's one thing," she whispered into Bennet's anxious ear. "Your brother's neighbors. They'll be gossiping about his guest. Someone's sure to mention the new arrival to the servants at the Manor."

Bennet, momentarily disconcerted, came back triumphantly. "We'll tell Richard—and the villagers—that you're a widow of a soldier killed in America—I've heard you talking about the war there. That'll explain how you come to know something about the place—and your accent, Miss Kathryn, which is not at all the London speech, if you'll pardon me for saying so."

Kathryn found courage to smile. "Bravo, Bennet! What a scenario writer you'd have made! Being a widow will give me a chance to wear a heavy veil—which I've no doubt you can provide me with! Your staff work is as fine as your powers of invention."

Bennet was delighted with the praise, but said firmly, "We'll fun about this when we have you safe at the farm, Miss Kathryn. If anyone questions you, you can say that you and your deceased husband being orphans, both of you, you'd no folk to go to in London, and I've sent you to board with my brother, since I knew your mother long ago."

Kathryn entered into the spirit of the scheme. "I could be a deaf-mute," she suggested, "and communicate only by writing on a slate. That would hide my accent, and it really ought to discourage casual questions—"

Bennet was forced to smile, but she said firmly, "Now then, Miss Kathryn, you're being whimsical. Not that you aren't in the right of it, at that! There's few enough of them Croftoners can do more than scrawl their own name, to say naught of writing out impudent questions."

Kathryn smiled. "I'd just nod, or point, or shrug, or whatever seemed appropriate, and smile sweetly."

"Oh, dear, that's going to be our problem. Any woman who looks like you do will be a nine-days' wonder for the whole county. They'll come to gawk at you, and someone's sure to recognize her ladyship."

"I never would have believed I'd have trouble because of being too beautiful," smiled Kathryn. "But that's easily fixed. I'll cut this very noticeable hair short, dye it black—we'll have to get some dye before the stagecoach leaves—"

Bennet wavered between horror and indignation. "Cut your hair? I suppose you'll cut your pretty nose off, too . . . oh, Miss Kathryn, it's wicked you're having all this trouble, and being driven out into the world, when it's none of your fault, whatever!" She began to cry.

Kathryn placed a gentle hand on the older woman's arm. "Come on, Bennet, you've given me such a wonderful way to escape being sent to Ireland, so far away from the portrait—" she caught her breath. "The portrait! Without it, I haven't a chance of getting back to New York!"

Bennet pulled herself together, blew her nose, and set herself to considering this latest problem. After a few minutes she said, "There's a way. I'll send the picture to Elsingham Manor. Lord John ordered the footman to 'store the damned thing out of sight somewhere.'" Bennet quoted primly. "I'll tell the man it's to go to the Manor. Then when it arrives, I'll have it hung in a room no one uses—and smuggle you in one night to—try again," Bennet concluded awkwardly. She trusted and pitied Kathryn, but she felt very uncomfortable with the idea that the portrait was a doorway into another place and time.

Kathryn was deeply grateful to this little woman, so loyal to the manchild she had been brought from Scotland to nurse, so grateful for his continuing kindness to her when he left her care. It was Lord John's father who had established the Bennets on the farm near the Manor, but it was Lord John himself who had begun the practice of bringing his old nurse to the great London mansion for a few weeks every year as a special treat. Of course Bennet adored him, thought Kathryn. The wonder was that she had not rejected Kathryn out of hand, after the gossip in the servants' quarters. Bennet was a just woman, enough of a pawky Scot to insist on making her own independent judgments. A compassionate woman, too, as Kathryn could testify.

"Bennet, are you sure you want to get involved in this? Lord John will be very angry with you if he finds out you have helped me defy his orders. He'll want to strangle both of us!"

"Then want must be his master," retorted Bennet stoutly. "That's a saying we have in my country, when someone says he wants something unreasonable. It means he's got to deal with his problem himself." She set her lips firmly. "I had little patience with tantrums when he was a child, and I have less now."

Kathryn chuckled. "Bennet, you're too much. And that's a saying we have in my country! But getting back to the plan: I've been wondering if the Manor won't be the first place Lord John will look for me, when he hears we've gone off together?"

"That's the beauty of it," Bennet explained. "We shan't go together. I'll whisk you out of the house and onto the stagecoach before anyone is up and about. Then I'll come back here. I'll be standing in the hall when they unlock this door and find you gone. I'll follow his lordship into the room, and pretend to find this note from Donner. Everyone will believe you've gone to Ireland with her!"

"Bennet, you're a genius!" said Kathryn, giving her a hug one-armed. "But I still can't agree to stay indefinitely with your long-suffering brother. After a few days I'll apply for a job in some large house in the neighborhood—"

"Doing what?" sniffed Bennet. "It's not likely you could manage heavy work, you being brought up like Quality, at a school and all. And you're far too pretty to be hired as a governess, even if you had letters of reference, which you have not. Besides, in any of the great houses, you'd be at hazard of meeting someone who's met—Lady Elsingham."

Kathryn was forced to agree. She sighed. "Very well, then. Help me dress and lead me to your stagecoach! You'd better write that letter to your brother. And you'll have to lend me the money for the fare, you know."

"I'd be happy to, Miss Kathryn, but you've got far more than enough in your reticule." She indicated a frivolous purse on the bureau.

Kathryn set her jaw stubbornly. "I shall not take one penny of That Man's money—" she began, but Bennet interrupted briskly.

"Then I shall, and give it to you. Now Miss Kathryn, don't be childish! Do you really think his lordship would be deceived for one minute if I said you'd gone off to Ireland without a penny in your pocket? Be sensible, Miss Kathryn, do!"

Kathryn smiled reluctantly. "Yes, Bennet," she said.

"Good! Now I'll help you dress, and then I'll write the letter to Richard, and then we'll smuggle you out of the house." She was bustling about as she talked, but she managed a surreptitious glance or two at the pale beautiful woman whose lovely face was drawn with pain and exhaustion. "I'll just pack a wee bag for you, Miss Kathryn: some underthings, a comb and brush, soap, and the laudanum Dr. Anders sent over to dull the pain and help you sleep."

Kathryn, dressed in what she suspected was Bennet's best dress and cape, found them a very snug fit. A bonnet and heavy veil were carefully fitted over the glorious hair.

"I could be Jack the Ripper and no one would know it, with this disguise," whispered Kathryn. She was feeling lightheaded with pain and nervous tension. Bennet forced her to sit down while the letter to Richard was being written. Then, with Bennet in the lead carrying the neat satchel of clothing, the two women crept down the great stairway in the dark. Kathryn was almost glad she couldn't see the elegance and beauty of the mansion she was leaving so stealthily. She had never really belonged here—even Nadine had been an interloper—*and a fool,* Kathryn thought, angrily. To have all this—and throw it away! Into her mind, unbidden, unwelcome, flashed a picture of a tall, golden-haired man, asleep somewhere in a magnificent bed, the master of this house. Perhaps in sleep the angry, contemptuous frown would be smoothed away, and his face would be relaxed and kind...Bennet opened the ponderous front door cautiously. The foggy chill of predawn struck into the warm, scented hall. Shivering, Kathryn followed the older woman out, waited while she closed the door, and then hurried after her down the street

Nine

Kathryn was never able to recall that journey away from London without mixed feelings. She told herself, as the coach clattered and swayed over the cobbles of the London streets in the dawn, that she should be watching and listening and storing up impressions. What other librarian in the history of the science had had a chance actually to live in the country and time of her favorite authors?

As the coach lumbered out into the country, Kathryn had decided that England seemed much smaller than she had pictured it. And greener. The country air smelled so fresh that she almost forgot the dull aching of her arm in the incredible sweetness of it. As a matter of fact, however, the one, overriding, inescapable sensation she remembered was pain: physical pain from her arm, held in a sling and bound close to her body, and nagging unhappiness from her ambivalent feelings toward John Elsingham.

She hated him for his arrogance, for his stubborn refusal to consider her problem without prejudice. Yet she could not forget his gentleness with her, and the disturbing sweetness of his smile. What a fool Nadine had been, to throw away the passion and devotion of such a man! What could it have been that had seemed more enticing to her than an adoring husband, an honored name, a fortune? Locked into the boredom and misery of the long jolting ride, Kathryn considered for the first time what she had learned about Nadine.

A young Irish girl of good but impoverished family, raised with casual indifference by a sport-mad widower father and a scheming nurse. It was little wonder that so young a girl, so raised, would not have been prepared to deal with the challenges and pitfalls of an ultrasophisticated society. And as the possessor of unusual beauty, she would have been the immediate target of every unprincipled gentleman in Polite Society. Kathryn, remembering what she had read about the *haut ton* of eighteenth century London, concluded cynically that even some of the "principled" gentlemen would have found Lady Nadine Elsingham fair game. And her seduction a hilarious joke on Lord John.

And there was Donner. Always Donner, lurking in the background, doing whatever damnable thing she did with her drugs and her wheedling and her hypnotic flat black stare. Small wonder that a wilful, ignorant girl, manipulated from infancy by God knew what techniques for what unholy purposes—small wonder, indeed, that she had become the reckless wanton of the portrait.

At this point in Kathryn's musings, the carriage had jolted to a halt. Kathryn felt a sharp stab of fear as she noticed a tall, gaunt figure, wrapped like herself in a dark cloak, waiting to board the coach. But the figure turned to mount, and Kathryn saw it was a man. It was not Donner, the girl realized with relief, only to know a new fear a minute later. For how could she have accepted so quickly the idea that Donner could have known of her flight already . . . could be able to pursue and find her so easily? She was seriously attributing to the Irish peasant woman powers verging on the supernatural! With such a psychological advantage, Donner would be a dangerous antagonist. Kathryn shivered as the tall man shouldered his way into the crowded vehicle. The coach did not start up at once. Instead, the red, weathered face of the guard appeared at the still open door.

"We'll be stoppin' 'ere a matter o' twenty minutes to change 'orses and," with a heavily-emphasized wink, "let Tom Coachman refresh hisself. So if any o' you wants a bite o' breakfuss, now's yer time!"

Grumbling, most of the passengers climbed awkwardly down onto the dew-slimed cobbles and straggled into the inn. Only Kathryn and the gaunt stranger kept their seats. The man did not seem inclined to speak, and Kathryn was glad of it. She closed her eyes wearily, and tried to find a more comfortable position against the side of the coach.

After a few minutes there was a clatter of nailed boots on the cobbles. Kathryn opened her eyes. Redface was thrusting a great steaming mug of tea toward her with one hand, while in the other grimy fist he clutched a huge sandwich of thick slices of meat between two chunks of bread.

"It's for you, Missus. Yer Ma gi' me the ready to get ye a bite an' sup when we stopped to change. So here 'tis, as promised."

Voicing her thanks, Kathryn managed to accept the mug with her free hand, but she couldn't endure the sight or smell of the food. "Please, no. I am not well. Just the tea."

The guard shrugged and turned back to the inn, munching at the sandwich as he went. Kathryn sank back against the seat and worked the mug up under her heavy veil. The tea was scalding, black, and heavily sweetened. She managed to get some of it down, and after a moment began to feel the better for it. By the time her fellow-passengers came out to the coach, grumbling at the haste with which they had had to snatch their food, she had finished the tea and was in a slightly more cheerful mood.

The trip from that point was sheer misery. The coach had been overcrowded by the presence of the gaunt man. The roads became worse the further they got from London, so the coach lurched and jarred and swayed. After one particularly vicious jolt, which threw the fat woman next to Kathryn heavily against her, Kathryn briefly lost consciousness. Her plight did not attract attention, however, since, having said nothing during the trip so far, her silence was not remarked. And since her face was concealed by the veil, and she was wedged so tightly between the fat woman and the side of the coach that she was fixed in an upright position, no one realized that she had fainted.

For the rest of the trip she was in limbo—half-dozing, grimly enduring the pain, quite oblivious of either her companions or the scenery. Eventually, about twelve hours after they had left London, the guard helped Kathryn to descend before a large inn which boasted the sign "GEORGE AND HORSE." He got her satchel out of the boot for her, pointed the way down the pleasant, almost empty street to a small, white building set back from the road.

"Yonder's Crown Inn, Missus."

Kathryn tried to thank him for his kindness as she pressed a coin into his hand, but he was already turning away to close the coach door and mount to his seat.

She trudged down the street, clutching on to the last of her strength. "Just to the Crown," she told herself. And then, "Just till I speak to the landlord, and give him the letter to Richard Bennet..." She held on grimly to the promise of a quiet room and a bed that would not jolt or sway. But there was a further challenge. Kathryn was met at the door of the inn by a large female with a very hard eye.

"Yus, Missus, what can we do for you?" she said, glowering suspiciously at Kathryn's plain dark cloak and veil, and the single satchel she had just set down.

But Kathryn had had it.

"I want," she said in a voice made harsh by pain, "a private room—the best you have—and dinner later, when I ring. You will also have this letter delivered to Farmer Bennet, if you please. You may give the boy a shilling and put it on my account. And now you may bring my satchel and show me the way to my room."

The landlord's wife knew when she had met her match. Quality! Didn't she know the haughty sound of them, riding roughshod over everybody! But no matter how odd they looked or acted, they paid their shot. She had not failed to notice the bulging reticule, and if the plain traveling cloak was not an expensive one, the lady's elegant shining boots more than made up for it. She therefore took the satchel and led the way to a clean, airy room on the second floor. It was her finest room, and she started to say something about its excellences as she ushered Kathryn into it, but again the guest forestalled her.

"This will do," Kathryn said. "I'll ring when I'm ready for dinner."

Whether it was the voice, or Kathryn's air of authority, or the formidable veil which did the trick, Kathryn never knew. But the landlord's wife left the room at once and closed the door quietly behind her.

Pausing only long enough to lock it, and to throw off the bonnet and veil and the heavy cape, Kathryn staggered over to the bed with her last ounce of energy, sank down into its feather-softness, and lost consciousness.

It was full dark when she opened her eyes. The leaded windows were open. Kathryn drew a deep breath. Delicious! London air had never smelled—abruptly she oriented herself. New York, she reminded herself grimly. New York's your home, not London. Don't let it get you, Kathryn, this flower-sweet air and the quiet peace, and the people. Bennet, yes—but there's Lord John and Donner, too. There's love here, but there's danger and hate. Don't you ever forget that! Your business is to lie low until you can get to that portrait. It's your one link with home—with reality. Now, pull yourself together, Kathryn Hendrix, librarian, of New York, U.S.A.

She found and lit a candle on the bureau, and was trying to wash her face, one-handed, in a china bowl, when she heard a light tapping on the door, and a cautious voice calling, "Missus Radcliffe! Are you awake, ma'am?"

'Radcliffe?' Just for a split second, Kathryn's mind lurched. Then she recalled that Bennet had written her brother to ask for Kathryn by the name of Radcliffe. What a sensible idea that had been! Her own name would have provided a clear lead to anyone searching for her near the Manor. She went over to the door, but didn't open it.

"I am awake," she called out. "Who is it? What do you want?"

"Ma'am, it's the chambermaid. Farmer Bennet is here to see you."

"Good," said Kathryn. "Ask him to await me in the parlor—you do have a private room downstairs?"

"Oh, yes, ma'am," the maid answered proudly.

"Very well. I shall be down shortly. Please instruct the cook to serve a plain, hot meal, and to set the table for two. Mr. Bennet will be my guest."

The maid clattered away down the stairs, and Kathryn began the awkward process of making herself presentable with the use of only one arm. Her hair was a tangled mass. Opening the satchel, Kathryn found a comb and brush and tried to tidy it. Hopeless. She searched for and discovered a pair of scissors in the satchel. Evidently Bennet had accepted the necessity of removing the glorious mane even if she hadn't been able to bring herself to do it.

Now Kathryn cut and snipped away until the shining red-gold mass lay all around her feet, and the pale face of Nadine, framed in a boyish bob, stared out at her from the speckled mirror. The pale green eyes looked even larger under the halo of curls; the piquant nose and sensuous lips seemed even lovelier in the youthful frame. Hastily sweeping up all of the tresses she could discover in the inadequate light of the single candle, Kathryn wrapped them in an undergarment and hid them in the satchel to be disposed of later.

Then she tidied herself as well as she could, put on the bonnet and veil and cloak, and went down to the parlor to meet Bennet's brother.

A big, heavy-set man stood before the fire, facing the door. He had a solemn craggy face topped with sandy hair, and the roundest blue eyes Kathryn had ever seen. He advanced toward her, and Kathryn had the fleeting notion that one of his own Scottish mountains was looming over her. In one huge, work-roughened hand he held Bennet's letter.

"Ah'm Reechard Bunnet, at yer sairvice, mu'm," were the sounds that rumbled from the man. "Ond ye must be the leddy fra Amurica." And while she was translating this into English, Richard Bennet smiled.

At that moment Kathryn would have put her hand in his and walked across the world. For Richard Bennet had a smile that would charm the fish from the streams. The craggy face was illuminated with incredible sweetness. She could understand his sister's praise. Without hesitation she went to him and offered her hand.

"Yes, I'm Kathryn Radcliffe. And I've come to stay with you, if you'll have me." As she spoke, she lifted the heavy veil and put it back from her face.

Richard's smile slowly faded and his blue eyes opened wide. "Och, you're bonny, Mistress Radcliffe. You're the bonniest lass Ah've ever set eyes upon."

Kathryn was startled into a laugh. "You come right to the point, don't you? That's the nicest thing anyone's said to me for a long time." She dimpled up at him. "There's a rumor that the Scots are a dour and taciturn race, but that's an obvious falsehood, I see."

Richard grinned. "Och, now, Mistress Radcliffe, normally Ah'm the dourest and most taciturn of men— Ah'd never use two words when one would suffice—but Ah'm just that knocked over by meeting you that my whole nature's changed entirely. From now on," he concluded, smiling down at her, "Ah'm sure to be known as 'that garrulous Scot.'"

Kathryn chuckled, but she felt compelled to look away from the open admiration in his face. She noticed the table set for two, and motioned that he join her there.

"Shall we sit down? You have read your sister's letter. Are you willing to help me?"

"Maggie has her wits about her, Mistress Radcliffe. If she says you're to be taken to the farm, that's where you'll go. She's an awful tyrant, our Maggie, in a nice quiet way. I doubt not that it's associating with the Quality has done it to her." The blue eyes were twinkling at her. "Och, aye, she's a managing woman, is Maggie, but she's always right. See what she's sent me this time!"

"Mr. Bennet, you are a flirt—"

"Call me Richard, ma'am."

"And a deceiver," continued Kathryn inexorably. "That very charming but almost unintelligible Scots burr seems to come and go as you need it. Now we must be serious. There are reasons why I must keep out of sight—keep a low profile, as we say where I come from. I'll put this veil back on now until our meal is served; then can we lock the door while we eat—and talk?"

Richard Bennet was serious at once. "No one will intrude, ma'am, if you so instruct."

"Very well." Kathryn replaced the veil and rang the bell on the table. A kitchen maid brought in a huge tray loaded with meat and vegetables. When she left, Kathryn lifted her hand to the veil, but a gesture from Richard stopped her. In a moment the girl returned with a second load of food and drink which she set on a sideboard. Then she stood waiting. Kathryn said gently, "This is very appetizing, thank you. I shall ring when I need you."

The girl bobbed a curtsey and scurried out.

Richard gently lifted the heavy traveling cape from Kathryn's shoulders and then seated himself beside her. She put back the veil and looked at the food on the table.

"I'll cut your food for you, ma'am," said Richard.

Kathryn felt a giggle of mirth rising in her throat. The huge man sounded so like his tiny sister. She smiled. "I can see I've come to the right person," she said. "What did your sister tell you in the letter?"

"You may read it, ma'am, later. Just now you should try to eat a little."

He worked deftly with knife and fork, selecting and carving choice tidbits for her plate. It was heartwarming to be treated like a small child, protected and loved, and she basked in the feeling. Under his gentle coaxing, she hardly realized how much she was eating, but finally she relaxed against the chairback and smiled at him.

"Enough, Richard! You'll make me fat!"

The big man, who had managed to stow away a formidable repast in spite of his close attendance upon her needs, sat back also and regarded her soberly. "To business, Mistress Radcliffe."

"First, is it an imposition for me to stay at your farm? Your sister said you wouldn't mind, but I'm thinking now of your reputation in the county."

His smile emerged. "No fear of that, ma'am. I'm notorious for picking up waifs and strays," he said, outrageously. Then, at her involuntary laugh, he went on, "There was a widow-lady with her wee bairn stayed at the farm last year, and a poor scholar-body of Oxford College, who was ailing from too much study, the year

106

before that. My sister sends them, or Lord John does, or others in the family. We've a fine large guest room, and a verra rrespectable cook-woman" (rolling his r's), "name of Cameron, who lives in the house and sorts us all. We're so respectable it's painful," he ended with a sheepish smile.

Kathryn was laughing again. "You've relieved my mind, Richard, and since I'm supposed to be a respectable widow-lady myself, I'll do no harm to your reputation."

He nodded agreement, his round blue eyes bright. If he had caught the "supposed to be," he made no comment.

After a moment, she went on. "I'm not sure how much your sister told you, but I've got to stay hidden in the neighborhood of Elsingham Manor for a little while, and I want to earn my living so I can pay you for my—"

She silenced his instant protest. "You must allow me my pride, Richard. I have reasons for not wanting to spend any more than I must of this money." She indicated the bulging reticule. "So I will ask you now: is there anything on your farm or near it—I would rather not go into Elsinghurst Village itself—that I could do?"

"Your arm is broken," he said, more reminder than question.

"Yes, but it's healing quickly. A few more days and I can take off the splints."

The man nodded. Kathryn liked it in him that he did not offer further argument or protest. He obviously knew what it was to have to earn a living, and he had his own pride. After a moment's thought he asked, "What can you do then?"

"I can teach: French, elementary mathematics, ge-

107

ography, some history, English language and literature." She paused, held by the open admiration on his face.

"Och, Mistress Radcliffe, that's a grand list, indeed!" He said with a twinkle, "Can ye no do more?"

Kathryn smiled back at him. "Yes, I can, you outrageous Scot. I am a qualified librarian."

A new expression had wiped the humor from his face. "Librarian, is it now? And isn't that the grand news?"

"Does the village need a librarian? I mustn't be seen near the Manor, so I hope it's not—"

"The Vicar," said Richard. "He resides in a fine house, also the gift of the old lord, not five miles from our farm. He serves the spiritual needs of both Crofton and Elsinghurst. He is a gentle, fashless, scholarly old fellow, who can recite you the dates of the Punic Wars but can't tell you what day this is. He has a house full of books, and he's just inherited another library from an uncle who was as much of a bookworm as he is himself. The poor old man is pushed out of house and home with the sheer bulk of learning he owns. 'Tis obviously your Christian duty to rescue the poor wee man."

"But that's wonderful!" Kathryn exclaimed. "I'll go over and offer my services tomorrow! I can arrange his books, and shelf and catalogue them—"

"I mind hearing him say there's many of them in Latin and Greek," interrupted Richard. "Would you be having these languages by any chance?"

"I have a little Latin. No Greek."

"Still and all, the good man should be happy to have you with one ancient tongue," conceded Richard. "Now, will you come with me this night—I've a trap here and a stolid old cob will get you to the farm as safe as an

108

egg in a basket—or will you stay the night at the inn?"

"I'll come with you now, Richard. Maybe your cook will help me to bed. I'd just as soon no one here knew of my broken arm." She hesitated, then asked, "Will she talk about me, Richard? Tell everyone about my arm and what I look like?"

Richard said quietly, "Rest your mind easy about that, Mistress Radcliffe. Elspeth Cameron will have plenty to say to you in private, if you do aught she disapproves of, but she'd rather be boiled in one of her own kettles than talk about farm business to any Sassenach—that's you English," he explained with a grin.

"Not me," said Kathryn stoutly. "I'm an American." She got up, adjusted the veil and handed Richard her reticule. "Please pay the landlord for my room and the excellent meal. Ask the girl to bring down my things. I'm really too weary to climb the stairs again."

At once Richard got up and went out. She could hear him, low-voiced, arranging to have his horse put to, and paying the bill. In a moment the little chambermaid was back, holding Kathryn's satchel. "I put in your comb and brush, ma'am, and your soap in the silver box," she said, wide-eyed.

"Thank you. You must have" (what did they call it in the 1770s?) "a gratuity," Kathryn said from behind the veil.

The girl bobbed and smiled. "Mr. Bennet, he already give me money from your purse, ma'am, and some for the kitchen maid too."

"Good," said Kathryn, hoping Richard's beneficence hadn't turned her into a nine days' wonder in case Lord John ever made inquiries for a lady with a broken arm. Still, she'd hidden that fact, she was sure, and the veil had hidden Nadine's face. And the too-memorable hair.

Richard let her out and helped her into the small

two-wheeled carriage, stowed her satchel under the seat, and took his place beside her. The landlord, his wife, and the chambermaid all stood on the broad doorstep, waving them off, with the well-lighted inn looking cozy as a Christmas card behind them.

Kathryn had determined to ask many questions about the Vicar and the farm, but before she knew it she was fast asleep against Richard's shoulder, with his arm firm and gentle around her. And so she came to Bennet Farm.

Ten

She woke very early with the sound of cowbells sweetly discordant, and a very unmelodious voice raised in Covenanting hymns directly beneath her room. She stretched luxuriously. The bed was firm enough to give her support; the linen was sweet with lavender, which came to her nose in fragrant whiffs every time she moved. The windows in her room were small, with many tiny leaded panes. Ruffled white curtains moved in the gentle breeze from the open windows. The early sunlight flickered on them like flakes of gold.

Kathryn's gaze slid lazily over the coverlet, a cheerful bright patchwork in blue and white; the floor, of oak polished to a satiny glow and covered with hand-woven blue rugs; a big old fashioned dresser with a starched white cloth on the top of it, and a heavy armoire, or cupboard, occupying most of one wall. A tiny round mirror hung above the dresser, so high that one would have to go on tiptoe to see one's face. Kathryn's lips quirked into a smile. She would be willing to bet that the owner of the voice singing doleful hymns had chosen that mirror. Trust a dour Scot to avoid the very appearance of vanity! Plain living and high thinking for you, my girl, she told herself; and then, more soberly, it's what you're used to, Kathryn Hendrix, so you'll be right at home.

The words had a good ring. I've never really had a home, she thought, quite without self-pity, rather with a kind of self-discovery. Isn't it strange I should feel so much at home in this English farmhouse, two hundred years before my birth? A little shiver of unease ran through her. Don't get too attached to all this!

"Time I was up and about the business of earning my living." In a library, too! Even if it was a multilingual hodge-podge, the choice and inheritance of an unworldly eighteenth century clergyman, it should be fascinating and absorbing. And rather a change from the flesh-pots of high society in London...

Kathryn sat up abruptly, not liking the direction her thoughts were taking. What folly to remember a pair of gray eyes warm with emotion, a golden head bent to hers, a deep voice saying, "You cannot deny that we do have—something for each other?"

Whatever they had, thought Kathryn crossly, it was Nadine and John who had it, not Kathryn. She got out of bed so quickly that she hurt her arm. It was then she realized that she was wearing a nightgown—too short, but very voluminous. She couldn't remember putting it on last night—in fact, she couldn't remember getting to bed at all. The managing Elspeth Cameron had probably managed that. And if she were the doleful

112

singer, what had she thought of Nadine's nighties? Giggling, Kathryn slipped out of bed and padded over to the dresser on bare feet. She pulled open the top drawer. Yes, there were Nadine's seductive French wisps, a drift of sheer pastels, so light they seemed almost ready to float out of the drawer. Kathryn picked up a sea-foam green confection and held it to her chest over the heavy linen nightgown. She chuckled. If *Glamor* Magazine could see me now! She began to waltz slowly, singing under her breath, "In my sweet little Alice blue gown..."

"Sing before breakfast, you'll cry before supper," came a harsh voice from the doorway.

Kathryn whirled, snatching the pretty negligee away from her body. A short, heavy-set woman, whose black hair was pulled painfully away from her face into a tight bun at the nape of her thick neck, was standing just inside the opened door. She wore a black dress with a huge white apron over it. She came in without invitation and shut the door.

"You've no business out of bed in your bare feet, Missus. You'll catch your death of cold, and be an added burden on them that has to take care of you. Surely you ken that on a working farm" (her accent made "wurrrkin' fahrum" out of the phrase), "there's no extra hands to care for idle folk."

Well, thought Kathryn, drawing a long breath, if that doesn't discourage fun and games, I don't know what would! She walked slowly over to the bed, but sat on the side and looked directly into the beady black eyes of her challenger.

"I'm quite well enough to be up and doing," she said quietly. "I shall not cause anyone any trouble."

"Ye may tell that last to one who hasna seen your face and figure," replied her tormentor tartly. "Or observed you dancing and singing in your nightshift."

"Is singing forbidden on Bennet Farm?" Kathryn asked. "I was sure I heard someone belting out a very doleful hymn a few minutes ago."

If she meant to discomfit the lady who was most likely to have been the performer, Kathryn failed of her purpose. The new-comer said dourly, "Hymns are a different matter, Missus, as any decent Christian creature should know. And I had already broken my fast."

Well, thought Kathryn, I asked for it. Suddenly very thankful for the money in her reticule, Kathryn spoke with the poise of one who is paying his rent. "Are you the cook?"

"I am Elspeth Cameron, indeed, and I take care of the household while Mistress Bennet is absent. Which is most of the time," added the cook, with what Kathryn perceived to be considerable relish. "She's back and forth between the Manor and his lordship's fine London dwelling. His lordship's nurse, she was."

Kathryn realized that she was no match for this battle-maid. Since she would have to live with the woman for several days, at least, until Bennet could get the portrait to the Manor and arrange to have Kathryn smuggled in, she had better keep the peace. She would also need help in bathing and dressing until her arm was completely healed. Kathryn took another look at the sour, disapproving face of Elspeth Cameron, and shivered. She simply couldn't have those heavy hands on her body. She'd have to find a way to manage for herself. Perhaps—

"Is there a young girl in the neighborhood whom I can engage as a maid?"

The disapproving look deepened. "Is it an abigail you'll be wanting, then, Missus? I doubt there'd be one in this vicinity would suit a fine leddy. Mostly they're farmers' daughters, more used to milkin' and muckin' out the barns than fussin' with such stuff as that, yon," and she jerked her head at the peignoir with a sniff.

"I see I shall have to find one myself," Kathryn forced herself to speak calmly. "Thank you for coming up to waken me. I shall be down for my breakfast in half an hour." She turned away and went to the wardrobe to find the clothing she had worn the previous day. After a minute she heard the door close.

It was all of half an hour before she was able to descend the stairs. She had given herself a hasty, one-handed sponge bath. It had been very awkward getting into the unfamiliar clothing, and she had deliberately left off some of the more esoteric undergarments. Her hair had been easy: a few hard sweeps with the brush had sent it into an enchanting halo for the pale beautiful face. Kathryn felt no envy nor pride. It was Nadine's face; she could admire it without self-adulation. Gathering her courage, Kathryn went downstairs.

The farmhouse was very large, very comfortable, and very clean. It would take a pretty rash grain of dust to invade Elspeth Cameron's domain, thought Kathryn, following her nose to the kitchen. Well, if smell is any criterion, I'll be the best fed American tourist in all of England.

The food was delicious, but Kathryn had trouble with some of it. The porridge was ambrosial—heavy with coarse brown sugar and cream that was as thick and yellow as custard. The poached eggs were a tender delight, and the strong dark tea (did everyone in England drink it this black?) put heart into her. But she couldn't begin to cut the thick slice of ham one-handed, and she stared with dismay at the roast beef and the covered pie.

"Is there something wrong with the food?" challenged Elspeth.

"No," answered Kathryn honestly, "I've never tasted anything as good. It's just that I can't cut the meat with one arm."

"Och, then you'll surely be needing help, like I said," Elspeth nodded. "We can't have you wastin' good food. 'Waste not, want not' is my motto."

"You can save it for my lunch," said Kathryn weakly.

"Will you be able to cut it any easier then?" asked Elspeth.

"I shall tear it with my teeth," said Kathryn calmly. "Now if you will tell me where to go to find a young woman who would be willing to come to help me, I'll get out of your way."

The pompous sentence had its effect. Elspeth said almost placatingly, "What-all would you be wantin' from the girl? There's none of them up to maidin' a fine lady."

"I shall need some help in dressing myself until my arm heals, which should be by next week," Kathryn enunciated clearly. "Also in cutting my food, as you have remarked. And I shall need a young woman with enough skill to make me a few simple dresses to work in."

Elspeth's eyebrows rose. "That last would be a sensible proceeding. You really intend to seek for employment?"

"I am a qualified librarian and am also competent to teach children," Kathryn retorted.

"'Tis few of the gentry would have you to instruct their bairns," Elspeth told her.

"And why not?" snapped Kathryn.

"Because of the very strange way you have of using

the language," explained Elspeth, smugly.

Since her own sentence had come out sounding like: "Becos o' the vayahry sturrange way ye hae o' usin' the longwidge," Kathryn found herself grinning, her good humor restored. "You and me both, Elspeth," she said. "We're nothing but a pair of foreigners among the Sassenachs. Now give me the directions to find a suitable maid."

She thought, as she walked along a green lane in the fresh morning sunlight, that Elspeth could very easily have sent her on a wild-goose chase. The small black eyes had still been hostile as she gave directions. But eventually Kathryn came to a neat, white-painted gate hung between white posts, just as Elspeth had described. She followed a wide track toward a prosperous-looking farmhouse. She was already feeling too warm, since she had donned Bennet's cloak and bonnet. She had decided not to wear the veil.

"They'll all have to see me sooner or later," she thought. "Better not to make a mystery. I'll get a white mob cap and wear it all the time over this hair. Or would black be better?" There was an unpleasant feel to that idea. Where had she—oh! Donner's white face closely encased in a black cap like a helmet. Well, she wouldn't wear anything like that. Maybe she'd show these English something new in widow's caps. Smiling faintly at that idea, she went, still following Elspeth's instructions, around to the kitchen door at the rear of the building.

There was a cheerful sound of women's voices and the clatter of pots. At her knock, one comfortable voice rose above the rest. "Hush now, girls, you're like a treeful of starlings with your chatter!" and then, louder, "Come in, Sarah!"

Kathryn pushed open the door. All sound abruptly ceased. A fat motherly woman came toward her, wiping floury arms on her apron. "I'm sorry, I'm sure, ma'am. We were expecting our friend from Crofton—"

"I wish I were she," said Kathryn. "I'm Kathryn Radcliffe, and I'm staying at Bennet Farm for a few weeks."

"Please to come in, ma'am! Poll, dust off a chair for Mistress Radcliffe! This way, please—or perhaps you would prefer to sit in the parlor? The farmer's wife was flustered, but seemed genuinely hospitable.

"Thank you! This chair will be fine. You all sounded so happy as I come along. Please don't let me interrupt!"

The cluster of pretty girls staring at Kathryn with avid interest now broke into a chorus of giggles, except for one slender miss with soft brown eyes. "Oh, hush up, you ninnies! Mother, can't we offer Mistress Radcliffe something?"

"That we can, Polly. Ma'am, would you fancy a cup o' tea?"

"I'd love a glass of cold water," confessed Kathryn. "The walk made me thirsty."

At a glance from her mother, Polly ran to fetch it, and brought it carefully. The glass was sparkling clean and the water cool and clear. Kathryn sipped it slowly, trying to observe the girls without seeming to stare. There were five of them, all fresh-faced and clean and wholesome; the youngest possibly twelve or thirteen, the oldest, the one with brown eyes, probably seventeen or eighteen. They had been making bread and cookies, and the kitchen was full of mouth-watering odors.

All the women stood watching Kathryn, their faces smiling and friendly. Kathryn handed the empty glass to Brown Eyes. "You are Mistress Bradley, are you not? And these are your daughters?"

The buxom woman beamed at her brood. "Indeed ma'am, they are, every one. And a help to their mother, if I do say so as should not."

"But you should," smiled Kathryn. "Mrs. Cameron tells me they are the best behaved and most accomplished of all the young women in the district."

"Did she, then?" marveled Mrs. Bradley, and the young girls went off into another spasm of giggling. "She's such a sour body, I'm surprised she spoke so civil."

"She told me," pursued Kathryn, "that all your daughters could cook and wash and iron, and that the eldest, Polly, was an accomplished seamstress as well."

Polly's pretty face became pink with pleasure.

"She said no less than the truth," boasted the farmer's wife. "Our Poll is a wonder!"

"Then would you," coaxed Kathryn, "permit her to come to the Bennet Farm daily to help me? I have had an accident with my arm, and I'm still very awkward. Also," she hurried on, afraid of a rebuff, "I need several neat, simple black dresses and caps to be made at once. I am," she concluded, "recently widowed."

This latter intelligence wiped all the smiles from their faces, and set them to murmuring condolences. Kathryn kept her eyes on the farmer's wife. "Could you spare me Polly for just a week or two?" She turned to the girl. "If you would care to come?"

The brown eyes were sparkling with excitement. "I would care to come very much."

Her mother appeared pleased but dubious. "She's had no training to maid a lady, ma'am. Nor to make such fine stylish gowns as you would wish to wear—"

"Plain, simple and sensible," corrected Kathryn firmly. "Suitable for a working widow." She noted their surprise, and added rashly, "I am going to catalogue

119

the books in the Vicar's library. That is sure to be dusty work. No place for a fine, stylish dress," she added with a smile.

Mrs. Bradley chuckled richly. "If you can find the shelves for the clutter, and locate the Vicar himself long enough to give you directions! He's God's good man, indeed, but he's the most forgetful, most helpless—" She shrugged. "I've been in the vicarage, times, helping Missus Latchet to clean it. Vicar lets her in once a week, if she reminds him, only he warns her not to move a single volume, lest she lose his place in it!" She laughed. "A regular rat's nest, it is, with more books than you'd believe there were in the world, stacked on every table and chair, and on the floor— and even on the windowsills! And every one of them— as you'll see!—with a paper or two stuck in to mark a page!" The good woman shook her head admiringly. "Do you suppose he's really read them all?"

Evading this, Kathryn said, "I hear he's just received another whole houseful of books from a relative, so I consider it my Christian duty to help him put them in some sort of order."

"You'll never do it," chuckled the farmer's wife. "But I can see you'll need our Polly to help you try! You'd better plan to take her to the vicarage too, for you'll never be able to straighten out that mess with one arm!"

"Oh, thank you, Ma!" breathed Polly. "When shall I start, Mistress Radcliffe?"

"Would today be too soon?" asked Kathryn, to everyone's amusement. The arrangements were easy to make, the most difficulty being encountered over the sum suggested by Kathryn for Polly's wages, which everyone, including Polly, said with a scandalized air was far too much. Kathryn hastily agreed to the miserable pittance which Mrs. Bradley thought adequate, and then made inquiries as to where suitable material could be bought. And would Polly need a pattern?

An agreeable hour was spent in dealing with these important matters. Mrs. Bradley agreed to buy the materials and all else necessary on the following Saturday, when her husband was to drive her to Elsinghurst market for supplies. Money changed hands, and everyone involved felt that a most satisfactory bargain had been made.

Walking home with the promise that Polly would wait upon her early the following morning, Kathryn felt that she was doing very well indeed in the new situation. The money in the reticule was going rapidly, but she had very little fear that she would not get the job. If the Vicar was that absent-minded, he might even think he had sent for her himself. Everyone agreed that he needed help desperately, and Kathryn was equipped to give it. Better, she thought with a little pride, than anyone living in this country at this time! So things were going satisfactorily, and as soon as Bennet had the portrait installed at the Manor, the way would be open . . .

Daydreaming thus, she was completely unprepared for the iron-faced woman who met her at the Bennet farmhouse. In one hand Elspeth held a long glowing lock of red-gold hair—held it as though it were a viper.

"Mistress Radcliffe, is it?" she hissed at Kathryn. "The chambermaid at the Crown Inn brought this. She says she found it under the bureau when she was cleaning the room you used. The silly fool thought it was so pretty it must be a keepsake belonging to the Widow Radcliffe. But we know whose head it came from, do

121

we not? From the head of his lordship's Irish hussy, Lady Nadine Brionny!"

Then, when Kathryn did not answer, Elspeth said triumphantly, "We are not all as easily hoodwinked as Richard Bennet is!"

Eleven

Several hours after Kathryn had left London for Crofton, Lord John came striding down the hallway toward his lady's bedroom. He had passed a miserable night. For a while he had been unable to get to sleep, rehearsing in his mind the things he had said, and hadn't said, and should have said, to that beautiful devil he had so foolishly married. Icy rage alternated with corrosive contempt, to be succeeded at length by the blackest despair he had ever known.

When finally he dropped into an uneasy sleep, he had a dream. In it, his door opened and a radiant Nadine came to him, her lovely arms open, such loving promise on her face as he had never seen even during their honeymoon in Paris. He had leaped out of bed to take her in his arms. Just as he was about to kiss her, her face changed and became...

He awoke with a cry, not knowing whether the face in the dream had horrified or delighted him. It was past ten o'clock. He had intended to rise much earlier, dress, eat, and then escort his wife to Ireland, by force if necessary.

He ordered his hovering valet to pack for a short trip, sent an order to the kitchen that a light breakfast was to be brought to her ladyship's room in half an hour, sent another message that a footman was to be despatched to procure two tickets for the Irish mail packet, and that his traveling coach was to be ready to leave within the hour. He called Paget back one final time, ordering him to notify one of the maids to attend her ladyship in fifteen minutes. Then he dressed himself and went to his wife's room.

As he strode down the hall, he was trying to banish from his mind the uneasiness which the dream had left with him. He took the key from his pocket and unlocked milady's bedroom door. In an instant all memory of the dream was gone. The room was empty. He went into her powder closet, even opened the huge armoire he had bought her in Paris—"large enough to make love in," she had said, teasing him. She was not anywhere.

His furious glance lighted upon Bennet, entering the bedroom with a solemn face, and his anger found an outlet. "Where is she?" he demanded. "How did she get out? I thought I told you she was to be left alone—!"

"Is her ladyship gone, then?" asked Bennet calmly. "Is that a note she's left you?" Walking quickly to the bed, she bent and picked up a folded paper lying partly under the ruffled valance.

"Let me see it!" snapped his lordship.

She handed it to him and watched as he read it.

"She's gone to Ireland with that creature!" he said, anger mingling with another emotion he refused to identify. "Well, good riddance. Of course I'll have to make sure she really gets there, and doesn't turn up in Brighton or Paris to dishonor my name further!"

Bennet surprised him. "Take shame to yourself, Master John," she said in the very voice he remembered from his youthful escapades. "You've driven that poor pretty child right into the arms of the wickedest creature I ever knew."

"Driven her! She was running to perdition before I ever laid eyes on her—and God knows how many she's corrupted on her way! I know of two she's worked on—Randall Towne and yourself! Didn't I see you with her just a few hours ago, working black magic with her damnable drugs?"

"For shame, sir! 'Twas a poor bewildered child trying to find herself, and I there to show her, as gently as I could, where her true place was. Look you now, Master John, the 'damnable drug' I was giving her," and Bennet held out the little brown bottle. *And I hope the good Lord forgives me,* she thought, earnestly, *for I know what I know and I'm trying to do things for the best.*

Lord John was looking at the bottle. It was empty, dry, and clean.

"I washed it last night," volunteered Bennet, without mentioning what time.

Lord John stared at it, sniffed, upended it, then threw it in a corner. Bennet was going to chide him for this show of childishness, but a careful look at his face dissuaded her. She had never seen quite that look on his lordship's face, and she knew enough to be quiet.

Lord John was no fool, and he suspected a trick, but the evidence he had, pointed to the truth of Bennet's analysis of the situation. After a minute's thought, he glanced at her. "If Lady Nadine has in truth gone to join Donner, I shall have to follow and make sure she is safely settled at Brionny Keep."

"You'll surely not leave her ladyship in that creature's care?" protested Bennet.

"Of course not. I'll give the woman over to the nearest magistrate for trial, and then set up a decent couple, man and wife, to look after her ladyship. I planned to do so all along." He turned away wearily, to meet his valet who was hurrying along the hall. "Well, Paget?"

"Everything you ordered is in train, sir. Your breakfast, your traveling coach, your luggage packed and stowed in your coach, the tickets for the Irish Mail will be here by the time you've eaten, and a maid has her ladyship's tray prepared—" He broke off to look past Lord John to Bennet standing in the center of the room.

"Thank you, Paget. You have been as efficient as ever," said Lord John quietly. "Her ladyship has already left. I shall be meeting her at the dock." His face was calm and imperturbable, as was Paget's, but Bennet wondered with a sudden pang how many times Lord John had had to make just such quiet-voiced excuses, and to whom.

"Lord Peter and Mr. Towne are here, milord," said Paget. "I asked them to wait in the morning room. Shall I tell them you are engaged?"

"No, I'll see them," said Lord John heavily. He turned to look over his shoulder at his nurse, and tried to smile. "Thank you, Bennet. You've helped me. And thank you for your kindness to—her. Stay here for a few more days and enjoy your holiday. It hasn't been a very pleasant one so far."

"God bless and keep you, Master John," whispered Bennet. "And her, too."

"Amen to that," he replied huskily, and went down to meet his waiting friends.

Over a breakfast that none of them ate, he shared as much as he had to of the problem which faced him.

"I would not speak of this even to you," he concluded grimly, "except that I need your help. That devil may not have taken Nadine to Ireland. If she's not at Brionny Keep, and I have to look elsewhere, I'd be glad of your assistance."

Lord Peter got up at once. "I'll go home and pack. Can you spare the time to pick me up on your way to Liverpool?"

"Of course. And you, Randy—will you enquire at the posting houses and at the ports for France? In case she's gone to Paris?"

"I will," said Randall, and went out without another word. Lord Peter hurried after him.

Lord John stared at the door through which his friends had gone. Then he put his head in his hands and sat at the table for a long time.

Twelve

Kathryn glared back at the woman who was obstructing the kitchen doorway. "Give me that!" she ordered, and took the lock of auburn hair from Elspeth's grasp. Pushing past the angry woman, she went to the open fireplace and threw the hair into the flames.

Elspeth gasped. If her ladyship was a witch as well as a brazen hussy, how dared she burn her own hair? Wasn't that a devil's trick witches used against their enemies? Her ladyship was coming back. Elspeth made the sign against evil which she had learned as a child. Her ladyship laughed.

"I should think a truly religious woman would be above believing in such superstitions."

"I am a true Christian, and I fear you not, either as witch or wanton!"

Kathryn controlled her anger. "Let us go and get your Bible, and I shall swear to you that I am not, in truth or spirit, Lady Nadine Elsingham, as God is my witness," she said quietly.

"Blasphemy!" Elspeth cried out.

"Nonsense. I am neither profane nor mocking. For a true believer, you seem remarkably forgetful. Let me quote two passages which seem to have slipped your mind. One is 'Judge not that ye be not judged,' and the other advises us, 'Judge not according to appearance, but judge righteous judgment.'"

Shaken but still holding to her anger, Elspeth muttered, "'The Devil can quote scripture for his own purposes.'"

Kathryn sighed. "Oh, Elspeth Cameron, can you really believe that I am that unhappy woman? What do you know of the dark forces that dragged her to her present state? Is there no pity in your heart for any creature?"

"I save my pity for them that merits it," said Elspeth. "If you aren't that hussy, what are you doing here?"

"I came because Bennet sent me, to give me a rest and a chance to heal my arm," began Kathryn.

Elspeth made an ugly sound of scorn. "Maggie Bennet is a fool. She lives like an innocent at the Manor, praised and cosseted and deferred to, in a pretty little world of her own. She vaunts herself on believing no evil of anyone, even if the same is proven and common knowledge. Every servant at the Manor knows better than to tell her anything that might threaten her image of her nursling—"

"And what could even the most malicious gossip say against his lordship?" demanded Kathryn with a heat that surprised herself.

"Och, so now you know his lordship, do you? I

thought it was only Bennet you were acquainted with," sneered Elspeth. "The gossip, as well you know, was about his lordship's wife, a red-haired Irish wanton, and his rash folly in so hastily wedding her, and the ugly scandals she has put upon him ever since. But you, Mistress red-haired Radcliffe of wherever you're from—you wouldn't have heard anything about that, would you?"

"I can only repeat what I have said," Kathryn reiterated wearily, cursing the day she adopted the name Radcliffe instead of her own. "I am not Lady Nadine. I am going to my room to rest. And you may do whatever you like." She turned and walked slowly up the stairway, leaving an angry, self-righteous woman behind her.

"I'll begin by telling Richard Bennet what I think," Elspeth cried out after her. "He'll know how to handle the likes of you." When the girl did not answer, Elspeth stumped back to the kitchen to prepare the evening meal. The fact that she was beginning to have doubts about her deductions did not sweeten her temper in the least. It was inconceivable to her that anyone as wicked as Lord John's wife was rumored to be could invoke the Holy Name so persistently without reprisal from on high. And yet—

Elspeth had hated the whey-faced, green-eyed creature from the moment that Richard Bennet had carried her into the guest bedroom in his own arms, and ordered her to undress the interloper and put her to bed. Those undergarments! No decent woman would be caught dead in them. Dead—! Elspeth sliced through a crusty loaf of bread with a savage slash of the big knife. To think that that creature should sit at the table across from Richard Bennet this night, and smile upon him, and stare at him out of those green eyes—

and eat the bread that Elspeth Cameron had baked with her own honest hands...! It was not to be borne! Be she Irish wanton or Colonial trash, it was Elspeth's clear duty to send her away from decent God-fearing folk!

And if she would not be sent? The thought struck Elspeth that the great baby, Richard, like all men, might be so bewitched by a pretty face that he'd refuse to throw her out. Then what?

It would be more than righteous flesh and blood could endure, to sit and watch her play off her tricks. But if she were not sent away...perhaps...? Elspeth gave the loaf one final, vicious slash.

When Richard came home, she was ready for him, presenting the image of her usual controlled self. She greeted him as she always did, asked and answered the usual questions. Only when he enquired after their guest did her voice raise a little. She told him of the lock of hair and stated her belief that their guest was none other than the Lady Nadine, up to some deviltry.

During her recital Richard's face became unusually stern. "If this is so," he said at length, "and our guest is that lady, I cannot perceive that it is any of my business—or yours."

"Not your business?" Elspeth repeated incredulously. "This is your house! Would you permit such a— person to remain here, knowing her reputation?"

"My sister sent her here for shelter. Surely she would know if—"

"Mag Bennet is as innocent as a babe unborn," protested Elspeth. "She's just fool enough—"

"Elspeth Cameron," said Richard quietly. She had never heard such iron in a man's voice. "This is, as you remind me, my house. The lady will stay here as long

132

as she wishes. Can you accept that? If not, then perhaps you should go."

Leave Bennet Farm? Leave its master? To her inner rage, Elspeth found herself cravenly agreeing to accept anything and anyone Richard Bennet ordered. The thought of being banished from this house was more than her spirit could endure.

Richard gave her his gentle smile, willing to forget and forgive, anxious to wipe out the memory of an unpleasant scene. But Elspeth Cameron, though silenced, would never forget.

Thirteen

Young Polly Bradley, introduced into the household at Bennet Farm as abigail, sleeping on a truckle bed in one corner of Kathryn's room, soon succumbed to a serious case of hero-worship. She was convinced that Mistress Radcliffe was the most beautiful, kindest, cleverest woman she had ever met. Poll very quickly learned, though, not to try to share her enthusiasm with Elspeth Cameron. That dour and formidable woman went about her duties with a face of stone, discouraging conversation.

Poll, wistfully hungry for knowledge, insatiably curious, had soon discovered that the lady she served had been to a *college*. Kathryn was the only woman she had ever heard of who had had that distinction. "But ma'am," Poll had said, "I didn't know them great places ever let a female in? Where was it you went?"

"It was called Radcliffe—and then I went to Columbia. Neither of them are in this country at all. They are in America."

"One o' them forrin places," sighed Poll, enchanted, as she continued to sew the dress she was making for her mistress. She loved these quiet hours in the fine bedroom, working and talking with the fine lady. Her eager young mind was stretching under the stimulus of Kathryn's conversation, as the latter was well aware. Challenged by Poll's avid questions, she found herself discussing history and literature, quoting poetry, explaining Greek and Roman myths. She tried to force herself to remember where and *when* she was, and tell the child nothing which would harm or bring her into question among her contemporaries, if she should repeat it.

Kathryn was spending most of her time in her bedroom, coming down only for meals and the long walks she took for exercise. Elspeth's face was a constant grim reminder of danger. Kathryn had no desire to arouse any further suspicions, either of witchcraft or madness. But it was hard to resist Poll's youthful enthusiasm and admiration, so she permitted the girl to work in the room, and often read to her while she sewed, or told her stories.

"What was the name of that female creature who turned people into rocks, now, ma'am?"

"Medusa? She was one of a charming family called Gorgons. There were three sisters, and not pretty like you and your sisters. In fact, the Gorgons had serpents—live serpents—instead of hair. And they were so hideous to look at that anyone unfortunate enough to catch a glimpse of them was turned into stone."

Poll giggled. "Elspeth Cameron must have seen one

of them," she whispered. "Turned her mug to stone. I ha'n't never seen her smile once since I come."

"*Came*," Kathryn corrected gently. Poll had asked for help "with her talk," and the educator in Kathryn couldn't resist the opportunity. She carefully guided the girl's thoughts away from the subject of Elspeth. "You've nearly finished my dress, haven't you? You're so quick! And the fichu is very becoming!"

"It's lucky Ma thought to get a bit o' white," agreed Poll, easily diverted. "If you'll forgive me, ma'am, for gettin' personal, you're much too young and—pretty— for all this black."

"Flattery will get you anywhere," teased Kathryn. "Are you bucking for a raise?"

"Bucking? A raise?" Poll was bewildered by the unfamiliar terms.

"Plotting for a bigger salary," explained Kathryn, smiling.

Poll chuckled incredulously at this humorous idea. "You're teasing me, ma'am! Ma says it's way too much I'm getting now. She's afraid it will spoil me. Of course she takes all of it to put away for my dowry, so it's little chance I have of being spoilt by any of it!"

Kathryn laughed with her, but the words had touched a real worry of her own. The money in the reticule was almost gone. She would have to have work very soon, or let Poll go. She still had not heard from Bennet, nor, for that matter, anything about events in London or Lord John. Apparently the Bennets, as a family, were not voluminous correspondents. She decided to ask Richard this very evening about the job with the Vicar, and what had happened in London of late—oh, very casually!

They always ate all the meals in the huge, comfortable old farm kitchen. Richard at the head of the table,

Elspeth taking Maggie Bennet's place at the foot, the two unmarried men who helped Richard work the farm on one side, and Kathryn and Poll on the other. Richard had insisted that Kathryn be seated at his right. Elspeth, silent and stern-faced, was up and down serving throughout the meal, scorning offered assistance. That night, while Elspeth was clearing the table, and the young men were leaving the house for their own hut with many a shy glance at pretty Poll, Kathryn spoke to her host. She tried to keep her tone light.

"Richard, it is time I had gainful employment. Have you spoken to the absent-minded Vicar?"

He gave her his slow smile. "That I have, Mistress Radcliffe. When he heard your qualifications, 'twas all I could do to keep him from storming the farm at once. I advised him he'd have to possess his soul in patience till your arm healed."

Kathryn, very conscious of Elspeth's listening ears, said quietly, "I'd like to begin to work as soon as possible. I really need the money. Can you arrange for me to meet with him tomorrow?"

"I'll drive you over myself, tomorrow afternoon," promised Richard. "If you're sure you are well enough."

Driving along the green lanes behind the sedate old cob, Kathryn felt a sense of relief. It was good to be heading toward work she loved and could do, good to be getting away from Elspeth's hostile presence. She had an idea.

"Does the Vicar have servants who live in the vicarage?"

"Yes, he has one old fellow, Newton, who cooks and looks after his clothing. The vicarage is large enough to house a half dozen, but Vicar lives plain. Oh, there's Mrs. Latchet, from Elsinghurst Village. She comes in once a week to clean up." Richard chuckled. "I don't envy the poor woman. Vicar absolutely forbids her to touch a single book or paper, and she says there's no level surface in the whole house that isn't covered with one or the other, or both!"

Kathryn joined his laughter. "Wall-to-wall books? I'll feel right at home. And that reminds me. It's time I found other lodging, closer to the vicarage. No," she halted his protest, "I can't be taking you away from your work, letting you drive me to the vicarage every day. You know that."

"I'd not mind," said the big man quietly. Alarm bells rang in Kathryn's mind. She continued firmly.

"It would be very much easier on me if I lived close to my work. Do you think—could it be arranged—that I could stay at the vicarage?"

Richard gave it careful thought. "There's enough bedrooms, surely—most of them full of boxes of books—," he grinned. "Of course it might cause talk."

"I couldn't have that."

"Perhaps if you took Poll with you?" Richard suggested. "She's young but she's steady. You might be glad of her strength, too. The place is a rat's nest—no fault of Mrs. Latchet. I'll swear the poor woman would be glad of a pair of young arms. 'Tis a big house, the vicarage."

Kathryn hesitated. "How much do you think the Vicar could afford to pay me? If I asked Polly to come with me, I'd need enough to pay her, too."

Richard grinned. "The Reverend Archibald Percy has enough to pay a dozen of you," he said. "The living was a gift of the old master, Lord John's father, and carries a generous stipend. Vicar gives most of it away, when he thinks about it at all. Mrs. Latchet pays the household accounts—otherwise the tradesmen would never get anything. Vicar has his mind on other matters."

"He seems to need an accountant as well as a librarian."

"The good man needs a manager," smiled Richard. "I can hardly wait till you see the inside of the vicarage."

When they entered the lovely old house a few minutes later, Kathryn decided she had never seen such an incredible confusion. The elderly manservant, Newton, ushered them past and around and through boxes of books, not yet opened, which usurped most of the spacious front hallway. With unruffled calm he led them to a sunny library at the rear of the house.

"Farmer Bennet and a lady," he said, and walked away.

The Reverend Archibald Percy received them with gentle courtesy, had to be reminded who Richard was, thought he'd met Kathryn before, asked her if she were his cousin Sophia from Bath, then looked again and announced with a broad smile that she couldn't be, because he'd just recollected that Sophia was his senior by ten years, and asked them to be seated.

While they were trying to discover chairs that had no covering of books, the Vicar seated himself, beamed at them, told Kathryn she was the most beautiful human being he remembered seeing, and asked them what he could do for them.

Patiently Richard reminded him that this was Mrs. Radcliffe, the widow who needed employment, and was a qualified librarian.

The Vicar stared at her, shook his head admiringly, and quoted, "'Behold, the half was not told me!'"

Kathryn, who had decided that she liked the gentle, aristocratic, white-haired old man very much, smiled demurely and said, "I believe that is *my* line, O King," and, indicating the huge piles of leather-and-gilt-bound books which filled every niche and corner of the room, she finished quoting what the Queen of Sheba had said to King Solomon, "'thy wisdom and prosperity exceed the fame which I heard.'"

The Vicar's gaze sharpened on her face and a slow smile of pleasure tugged at his lips. "Can I believe my ears? To our rustic hamlet have you indeed brought 'the feast of reason and the flow of soul'? Art thou Minerva, Goddess of Wisdom?"

Kathryn laughed. "Thank you, Father Percy, but I am neither Sheba nor Minerva. Merely Kathryn—Radcliffe of New York." Somehow it had been hard to give the wrong name to this good old man.

The Vicar focused on her lovely face. "You not only got my reference to Solomon, but you capped it! Refreshing! Very few, I may safely say almost none, of my parishioners could have done so. Well, well, so you are to be my librarian and set my books to rights." He pulled the bell-rope; then, without waiting for his servant to arrive, called "Newton! Newton!"

The old servant must have been waiting outside the door. He entered slowly, bearing in trembling hands a large tray, much tarnished, and three glasses and a decanter.

"Newton, I see you have brought the sherry. Very well done! But perhaps our lady guest would prefer tea. Have we any tea for Mistress Radcliffe, Newton?"

"I suppose I could make some," said Newton dubiously. "It's not Latchet's day, sir." He went slowly out of the room.

"We only have afternoon tea on the days Mrs. Latchet is with us," explained the Vicar. "Poor old Newton! He's got sadly set in his ways. We both have, for that matter." He smiled at Kathryn. "It will do us good to have you with us, my dear."

"I should like very much to stay here in your house with my abigail, if it would not be too much of an imposition," said Kathryn, striking while the iron was hot.

"Imposition? Nonsense! It would be a blessing," protested the Vicar. "I'm sure there is room. And you offer me the opportunity of conversing with a scholarly mind! What college was it you lectured at?"

"I am a graduate of Radcliffe College and Columbia University," said Kathryn. "They are both in America. I have not taught, but I have worked as a librarian."

The Vicar's eyes opened wide. "But this is most impressive! You'll want to get to work at once, I'm sure!" He surveyed the cluttered room lovingly. "All my dear friends! Every volume a cherished possession, Mistress Radcliffe. I know I need not warn you, a true bibliophile, to handle them gently. And not—perhaps—lose the places I have marked?" he said, a little anxiously. Then, reassured by her smile, "Good! I'll go help poor Newton with the tea. He's a good old fellow, but sadly slow and set in his ways."

Kathryn turned to Richard after he had left. "He is a darling," she said softly. "I'll enjoy putting his library in order for him. Thank you for arranging it. It is going to be all right, isn't it? My staying here with Polly, I mean."

Richard reassured her. "He'll love it. You heard what he said—someone to talk to who speaks his language. And Newton won't care one way or the other. The one you've got to win over is Mrs. Latchet. Why don't I take you to her home when we're finished tea—if we ever get it," he concluded, smiling. "What do you wager both those old fellows have completely forgotten us?"

But that was a libel. Newton appeared, tottering under the weight of an enormous tea tray. The Vicar asked Kathryn to pour for them, and enjoyed his tea so much that Kathryn resolved she would serve him some every afternoon. They took their leave soon after tea, Kathryn promising to return the following day to begin her work.

Richard drove directly to the cottage occupied by the Latchets. That good lady was at home, and so impressed by a visit from Mr. Bennet and his guest from the Colonies that she fairly glowed with excitement. She could scarcely be prevented from giving them a second tea. When Kathryn's new job was explained to her, Mrs. Latchet's face lighted up.

"You, ma'am, and Polly Bradley, going to stay with Vicar? That's the best thing I've heard since Christmas! Not that you'll have any comfort! The whole house is a rat's nest of books and papers, dust-catchers! and there's no woman born who could bring order out of it! Still, Poll's a well-trained girl. Her Ma's a friend of mine, and I've heard how kind you've been to Polly, ma'am, teachin' her and all!"

"I've been fortunate to have her," said Kathryn with a seriousness which endeared her to Mrs. Latchet. "She's a bright, well-mannered child, and an excellent seamstress. She does Mrs. Bradley credit."

Mrs. Latchet reacted warmly to this praise of her friend's daughter. "That she does, ma'am. Well, to think of little Poll at the Vicarage! If you're goin' to stay there, ma'am, I'd best get over first thing in the morning and clean out a room for you. Do you move in tomorrow?"

"Yes, and I thank you for your offer to help. I don't know how Polly and I would have managed to settle in without you."

Beaming broadly, Mrs. Latchet saw them to the door.

As they drove away, Richard glanced at Kathryn. "You've a nice way with you, Mistress Radcliffe. Mrs. Latchet will now consider herself your sponsor and ally."

"I'm sorry I couldn't establish an equally good relationship with Miss Cameron," said Kathryn soberly.

Richard frowned. "I can't think what's gotten into Elspeth. She's always been dour, but of late she's as threatening as a thundercloud."

"She'll be easier when she's rid of me and Polly," said Kathryn lightly. "We've been an extra burden."

Richard shook his head stubbornly. "It's more than that. She's got a bee in her bonnet." He frowned at Kathryn. "I'll never understand women," he confessed humbly. "Could she be jealous of you—Kathryn?"

The inner alarms rang wildly. Kathryn kept her voice warm and casual. "She's done an excellent job in charge of your home, Richard. It's unreasonable to expect that any woman so involved in running a large household could calmly accept two strangers and all the extra work that entails."

"I don't think that's it," insisted Richard. "We had Mrs. Hetherington and her child with us last year, and Elspeth wasn't like this. I cannot understand it."

"Well, she's sure to feel better as soon as Polly and I are safely settled at the vicarage," Kathryn said, and hoped very much that she was correct. Elspeth Cameron's hostility was a tangible thing, and disturbing. If only one could confide the truth to the gentle giant beside her! But it was too dangerous. The game she was playing was for her sanity. She must remain near the Manor until Bennet could get word to her that the portrait was there. And in the meantime, Richard Bennet must be held at arm's length—for everyone's sake.

Kathryn and Polly settled in at the vicarage with less difficulty than they had anticipated. When they arrived, Mrs. Latchet was already in the field, the Vicar had barricaded himself into his study, and Newton was in full retreat. Mrs. Latchet met them with a flushed and shining face, and sleeves rolled to the elbow.

"Come right up to your room, ma'am. Polly child, it's a good thing you'll be here to help! This place—!" Words apparently failed her. She had, however, accomplished a small miracle already, as Kathryn and Polly hastened to assure her. She had cleaned out a large bedroom, set up a small cot in an alcove, placed fresh linens on both the bed and the cot, washed the floor, and was busy dusting out the drawers of an old highboy.

"I haven't much with me." Kathryn indicated her satchel and the wrapped bundle of new dresses Polly had made her. "I came away from my home rather hastily, and had no time to pack more."

"The Colonies," agreed Mrs. Latchet as though she spoke of Outer Mongolia or Mars. "I'm told there's trouble brewing there, ma'am. 'Twas well you got away when you did. Now, Poll, you help your mistress settle in, and I'll get on with the luncheon."

"She used to work at the Manor," confided Polly proudly, after Mrs. Latchet had bustled happily away. "She was an upstairs maid, and got into the habits of the gentry. Luncheon at noon, and tea at four, and then dinner at all hours! As late as nine or ten at night, sometimes!"

As she prattled, she was putting Kathryn's things in the highboy, and hanging the new dresses in the wardrobe. "There now," she announced with satisfaction, "you're settled, ma'am. I'll just fetch up my own things, and get them put away."

"And I," said Kathryn, who had hung up Bennet's cloak and bonnet, "will get to work!"

"You look older, ma'am," commented Polly. "Very beautiful," she hastened to add, "but sorrowful. I reckon it's all the black." For Kathryn had had the girl make a neat dark cap to go over the glowing curls and hide every sign of them. The black dress was protected by a black washable apron which Kathryn hoped would catch most of the dust.

"Well, Polly, it's suitable attire for my job and for my station in life," she said. "Let's get to work."

Downstairs, Kathryn took her time in assessing the problem. The confusion in the house, she decided, was caused by two things. No book, once taken down, was ever replaced on a shelf; there were too many books for any building which also had to serve as a dwelling. Aside from the shelf-lined study, where the Vicar had prudently locked himself in, there was a room set aside as a formal library. There were bookshelves also in the parlor, and Kathryn suspected there would be more of them in the Reverend Archibald Percy's bedroom. Thousands of books! This was a noble holding indeed, and Kathryn's fingers itched to get at their task. But first things first. She requested a bucket of water, soap, and cloths from Mrs. Latchet, and began to wash the painted wooden shelves. Polly came at once to help, and by lunch time they had every shelf in the library and parlor clean. The confusion of heaped books was hideous, but Kathryn surveyed it with some satisfaction.

"We'll polish the shelves this afternoon, Polly. That'll keep the dust from settling again."

Polly agreed with all the fervor of her mother's daughter. Mrs. Latchet came to call them to lunch and surveyed the clean shelves with approval. "That's setting it to rights, ma'am! We'll maybe get this place in order after all!"

The whole house was redolent of furniture wax, and the shelves in the library and parlor were shining, before Kathryn and Polly, exhausted, called it a day. Mrs. Latchet announced that dinner would be served in an hour, and that the Vicar had requested the pleasure of Mistress Radcliffe's company at his board. Polly helped Kathryn wash, and took their dusty aprons with her to the kitchen. She was to have her meal there with Latchet and Newton.

Kathryn, whose whole arm and shoulder were one agonizing ache from the unaccustomed labor, was of two minds about going down to dinner. She looked longingly at the bed, so inviting with the crisp white sheets neatly turned back by Polly. Then she sighed. The Vicar obviously anticipated a pleasant evening, and she owed him that, at least, for the safe refuge he was giving her. She hadn't covered her tracks too well, she thought wearily. She'd asked Polly not to mention her red hair, but everyone at the farm had seen it, and Elspeth would be sure to volunteer the fact and air all her suspicions if any enquiry were to be made. Well, I'll just have to take my chances, Kathryn decided, and hope that no one comes looking for me. And then she wondered why she felt so depressed.

For the Vicar's sake, she put her worries behind her at dinner. He held her chair for her in the small, charming dining room which looked out through wide windows onto the lawn at the back of the house. With really touching courtesy he had forborne bringing a book to the table, telling her that live conversation

147

should be his treat this evening. Kathryn tried to match his courtesy gallantly.

"No, no, Vicar, I will not allow that a mere female can compete with Cicero and Vergil and Homer! Even Plato would only permit a few of them in his Republic."

"But you are forgetting the prime motivator of all good talk, madam." The Vicar's eyes twinkled, and he paraphrased: "'This was the face that launched a thousand ships!'" He bowed and raised his glass to her.

"You'll not win me by flattery, sir," Kathryn countered, racking her brain for a suitable rejoinder. And then she had it. "'I fear the Greeks, even when bearing gifts!'"

The meal proceeded in a glow of mutual pleasure. Kathryn found her exhaustion giving way under the blandishments of good wine and food. Since arriving in this time, she had never felt so much at ease, so truly happy. The challenge, when it came, was therefore the more devastating.

"My dear," said the Vicar gently, "I have not enjoyed such a dinner since I left the Commons at Magdalen College. But you have had an exhausting day, and I must let you retire to your room. May I say two things before you go?"

"Of course!" Kathryn smiled at him in the candle-glow.

"My house is blessed by the presence of such erudition and beauty combined—Venus and Minerva."

Kathryn found herself unable to answer.

"But my dear child," the Vicar went on gently, "there is no college in North America which admits both men and women. Who are you? If you are in trouble I sha count myself honored to be permitted to help you."

Kathryn stared at him, the blood leaving her cheeks. He brought her a glass of sherry, forced her to sip it, begged her pardon, castigated himself for a foolish old man. "My dear, forgive me. I did not mean to cause you pain."

"I shall tell you my story . . . but you will think me either mad—or—" She couldn't say it to this kind old man.

"Not mad," he said gently. "Never that."

"Or possessed of a devil!"

He came to her, took her hand, stared long into her eyes. She met his searching stare bravely until her own eyes watered and the tears flowed down her cheeks.

"Poor child," the old man said. "Who has hurt you so?" And he kissed her forehead gently. "Now tell me what is wrong."

Fourteen

Mr. Randall Towne was kicking his elegantly-shod heels in Lord Elsingham's library one evening when the door opened to admit the owner and Lord Peter Masterson.

"What ho!" said Randy, searching their faces. "News?"

"None," said Lord John. "You?"

"No sign of her at any of the Channel ports; no rumor in Paris. And you know, old fellow, that if she were there—"

"Yes," agreed John morosely. "The salons and boutiques would be buzzing."

"No luck at all in Ireland?"

"'Devil a bit,'" quoted Peter grimly. "I'll swear she never got as far as Liverpool."

"The dresser?"

"We heard that Donner had been back to Brionny,

151

but she wasn't there when we arrived," John said heavily.

Randy was too shocked by the expression on his friend's face to continue the discussion. He did have one slender clue, but before he shared it with this troubled man, he wanted to discuss the situation with Peter. Sound man, Peter. For all his great size he had plenty in his bone-box. Randy fidgeted nervously until Lord John sighed wearily. "We're all too tired to think straight. I'm going to bed. I'll see you both tomorrow. And about the help you've given me—you know how I feel—"

"Don't say it!" begged Randy, who had a horror of being thanked especially when he was concealing a clue which might wipe the desolate look off his friend's face.

As Peter and Randy went down the steps to Randy's waiting carriage, Peter said abruptly, "He hasn't slept a wink since we left London. Nor has he eaten enough to keep a bird alive. This is bad business, Randy."

"It's worse than that," said Randy gloomily.

"Why do you say that? And what in Heaven's name possessed you just now? You were as nervous as a nun in a crib."

"Don't be vulgar," said Randy. "The thing is, I think I know where she is."

"You think you know—!" began Peter incredulously. Then with a roar that startled an approaching pedestrian, "And you didn't believe it important enough to mention? Why, you miserable little cockerel—"

"Oh, be quiet," said Randy. "And use the brain you're supposed to have. If I'm right, and we find the lady, *then what?*"

Lord Peter gaped at him, then slowly closed his mouth. "Yes. I begin to see the dilemma. Has she run off with another man?" He enunciated a vicious oath. They had not been easy nor pleasant, these days spent with his friend in the fruitless search. "How the devil can we protect him from this bitch? Who is the man, by the way? Do I know him?"

Randy colored. "I don't know that there's a man involved, exactly... well, at least... there's got to be, wouldn't you say? I told you I got back from Paris yesterday. I came at once to John's house to discover if you two had returned from Dublin. Old Burl wasn't much help, so I waited for an hour or so, on the chance of news. While I was strolling around, I noticed that damned great portrait of Nadine was gone from the landing. I asked Burl what had happened to the portrait, and he said his lordship had sent it to the Manor. Well, I caught a flash of an expression on the face of one of the footman, so when old Burl had gone back to his pantry, leaving me to await a non-existent message from you two," he interjected sternly, "I bribed the footman to tell me why he'd got that silly conspiratorial look when Burl was talking to me. He said his lordship had sent the picture to the attic the night before you left for Ireland, and then, not ten minutes after you left, Bennet had told Burl his lordship wanted it sent to the Manor. The footman said he'd been in the hall all the time, and no such order had been given."

Peter was staring at his friend with annoyance and pity fairly evenly mixed. "Have you any idea what you are trying to say, or are these the ramblings of a mind overset by too much fine French brandy?"

"The portrait, idiot! Don't you remember John telling us he caught his wife and Bennet playing some jiggery-pokery in front of the portrait? That's why he had it sent to the attic."

"So?"

"So he surely wouldn't change his mind and have it sent to the Manor between the time we left him and the time he picked you up."

"Why not?" argued Peter.

"Because, for one thing, he hadn't time, and for another, he'd be more likely to want to forget the damnable, seductive thing than to parade it through every one of his houses! I should think that would be clear to the meanest intellect!" shouted Randy, exasperated.

"Not so much righteous indignation, young Jaw-me-dead," advised Lord Peter calmly. "You're attracting the attention of the hoi polloi."

Randall's coachman was indeed staring down at them with interest, and a passing nursemaid was casting amused glances at the elegant young bucks quarreling on the street. Lord Peter boosted Randall into the carriage and got in after him.

"You are right, little man," he admitted. "This does call for some thought. One of the less attractive things we learned about Donner in Brionny Village is that she is believed, by everyone who knows her, to be a practicing witch. They cross themselves when her name is mentioned."

"Superstitious lot, Irish peasants," offered Randall, not much struck by this.

But Peter persisted. "Not all of them were peasants, my lad. The parish priest told me she'd have been burned at the stake fifty years ago. 'And I'd light the faggots,' he told me. 'She's a creature of pure evil. We all breathed easier when she left. She is a child of the Devil.'"

"D'you think she's got her claws into Nadine?"

Peter shrugged. "I think it likely she's after her. I'm just not sure it might not be a good idea to let her succeed in her quest."

154

Randall considered that soberly enough. Finally, "I cannot agree, old man," he said. "She's been the evil genius behind all that's happened, if you can believe what you hear. It stands to reason she'll cook up more of the same, or worse, if she gets hold of Nadine again. And the girl *is* Lady Elsingham."

Lord Peter was frowning. "What I can't understand is dear old Bennet mixed up in this hell-brew. She was such a tower of strength and rectitude in our youth."

"Maybe Nadine or Donner has bewitched her, too," offered Randy. "Had we better tell John what we fear before something else happens?"

"If he doesn't get some rest soon, I won't answer for his health," Lord Peter said. "We'll wait and tell him first thing in the morning."

As the two friends entered Elsingham House the following morning, they encountered another visitor in the hall. Burl led them into the library, under the jealous gaze of the stranger.

"It's Mr. Manton, of Mr. Edmund Burke's staff. Most anxious to see his lordship. Says his mission is one of the utmost urgency," whispered Burl. In common with all Lord John's staff, Burl knew that matters were not well for his lordship. Burl was happy to place responsibility in the hands of his master's best friends.

"Is Lord John awake?" asked Randall.

"He is just coming down, Mr. Towne—or so Paget informs me."

"Then let's get out into the hall," decided Lord Peter, suiting action to word. As they came into the hall, Mr. Manton arose and fixed a reproachful gaze upon them. 'I was first in the field,' his expression said.

And then Lord John came down the stairs. He caught sight of his friends, and moved toward them, smiling. Mr. Manton fairly erupted into the group. Ignoring everyone but Lord John, he cried out, "Milord! I must see her ladyship at once! It is a matter of great urgency—involving national security!"

Lord John looked down into the angry, worried face. "My wife is not here at present, Mr. Manton. May I help you?"

"She must be brought here at once!" shrilled Manton.

"You forget yourself, Manton," said Lord John sternly.

The little man pulled himself together with an effort. "My apologies, milord. The matter is—of the utmost urgency. When I had the privilege of meeting her ladyship several weeks ago, she informed me—in your presence, sir!—of an encounter at Lexington. April 19, she said, milord!"

"I believe I recall something of the sort," Lord John answered, suddenly very interested indeed.

"It has happened! His Majesty's ministers have just received word of an action taken by the defiant citizens of Massachusetts, in which a detachment of General Gage's soldiers suffered heavy losses. I need not give details—" the little man glanced warily at the other men in the hallway, "but you can see that I must see her ladyship at once...and...you can understand why, can you not, milord?" He ended almost in a wail.

"By God!" said John Elsingham, "she was right!" and a smile spread over his face. He grinned at the astonishment on the faces of Lord Peter and Randall, then turned courteously to Wilmot Manton.

"I truly regret that I cannot give you a conference with her ladyship, but she has been ill and is in the country, recuperating. You recall she had just broken her arm when you saw her—"

156

"Yes, yes, but that must not be allowed to stand in the way. As a loyal Englishwoman, it must be her first responsibility to serve her country—"

Still smiling, Lord John interrupted him. "My wife is not an Englishwoman, and her responsibility—that is, she might feel—" He laughed, joyously.

Lord Peter moved in smoothly to soothe and divert the affronted Mr. Manton. "Lady Nadine is Irish, Manton, but what is more important, she's very ill. His lordship will agree to notify you when his lady is able to confer with you. And now I'm sure you will excuse us?" and he turned Manton over to the hovering butler.

When the little man had taken a reluctant departure, Peter herded John and Randy into the library and closed the door.

There was an expression on Lord John's face which his friends had never seen before. "She was telling the truth," he said softly.

Randy opened his mouth to object, but Lord Peter ruthlessly forestalled him.

"This little cockerel has used his head for once in his life. Randy, tell him about the portrait."

Randy repeated his discussion with the footman, who was promptly called into the library and interrogated. They got no more from him than Randy had already learned, but John, riding a wave of euphoria, decided it was enough. He sent the footman for Paget, and ordered that worthy to have the big traveling carriage around within twenty minutes.

"I suppose," he regarded his two friends with twinkling eyes, "you two will want to accompany me to Elsinghurst and offer your apologies to Kathryn," he said.

"I shall insist upon coming," retorted Lord Peter,

"if only to prevent you from making a fool of yourself. What is this about Lexington?"

"That's right, you weren't present when—when Kathryn announced that the first skirmish in the War of Independence would occur at Lexington on April 19. Since the day of her announcement was April 18, Mr. Manton, perhaps understandably, felt he was being hoaxed. It takes military intelligence from three to four weeks to reach us from the Colonies," he explained kindly.

Lord Peter was not amused. "You were fortunate he decided it was a hoax. A more imaginative man might have suspected—witchcraft."

"I will admit to a certain sense of urgency, in Manton's felicitous phrase," confessed Lord John. "My poor Kathryn down among the peasants. I hope she will have sense enough to keep her mouth shut."

Randall regarded his friend with anxious eyes. "Johnny, my good child, if your wife tells the villagers about coming back from the future, she's apt to be burned as a witch."

Lord Peter glared at him, but he insisted, "You know what English peasants are like, Peter. They're still living in the Middle Ages. Don't even know Queen Anne's dead! And the Scots burned a woman as a witch less than fifty years ago, on far less evidence than this. M'father told me about it."

"That's the dandy! Just keep reassuring us," gritted Peter, watching the smile fade from Lord John's face. "Johnny's beside himself already with worry—"

"No," Lord John said quietly, and stood up. "I'm clear in my mind at last. I believe her story. She's Kathryn Hendrix. I don't know how it happened, but I'm convinced Kathryn is telling the truth."

His two friends watched him in a troubled silence

as he paced the room, deep in thought. Finally, "What are we going to do about it, when we get down there?" Randy ventured.

"We're going to tell Bennet to produce Kathryn," said John with a return of the joyous smile. "I've a suspicion that more went to Elsinghurst than the portrait of milady."

Fifteen

Elspeth Cameron was having a particularly bad day. The bread had fallen into a doughy mess in the oven, the soup had burned, and the milk, left to cool in the ice house, had acquired a peculiar, bitter taste. Elspeth, grim-lipped, knew What Had Happened. Some evilly-disposed person was "over-looking" her.

Feeding her jealousy, she disregarded all the rational explanations for what had occurred, and convinced herself that the Witch of Brionny was attacking her. She debated whether to warn the Vicar—he was not of her faith, being High Church of England, the next thing to Popery in her Covenanting mind—but he was a decent, honest man, if gullible. He'd taken the Strange Woman in and let her run tame in his house. No telling what spells the witch had cast, what evil she had already done.

The villagers at Crofton and Elsinghurst, a gaggle of feckless fools, were forever praising the creature. What a fine piece of work she'd made of getting the Vicar's books in order; how learned she was for a woman! For nearly two weeks Elspeth had had to listen to it. The fools were even talking of asking the creature to set up a dame's school for their children!

"'A false prophet shall show great signs and wonders, so as to lead astray even the elect!'" Elspeth quoted grimly to herself. She loved the chapter in Matthew which foretold famines and earthquakes and the abomination of desolation. Well, she decided, the besom won't lead me astray!

Elspeth got her shawl, put it over her head, harnessed the cob to the trap, and set out for Crofton. First she'd talk to that Debbie at the inn, the girl who'd brought the lock of red hair. Likely she'd be able to tell how Mistress Radcliffe had arrived at the inn—who was with her—what had been said and done . . . Elspeth drove along the lane, oblivious of its fresh beauty, planning ways to discredit the witch.

Luck was with her.

She was talking to Debbie, asking her for every possible detail about 'Mistress Radcliffe's' arrival, when the London coach clattered past the inn, with its usual attendant racket.

Debbie twisted her hands together. "It's like I told you, Mistress Cameron, I found the one curl of pretty hair under the bureau, where I reckon Mistress Radcliffe dropped it. I truly got to go now! There goes coach, and Master be very strict about getting ready for custom!" She ran off, thankful to be away from her sour-faced inquisitor.

Elspeth, left standing in the inn parlor, debated the wisdom of staying longer in hopes of extracting further information. So far she hadn't got much. The woman had come alone on the stage coach from London. She'd been heavily veiled. She'd paid promptly and well. Would Lady Nadine Elsingham have ridden on a common coach? Not too likely. Elspeth glanced out the window. A tall, veiled woman clothed all in black was coming to the front door of the inn. Another of them! Was there a coven of witches gathering? With a thrill of pure horror, Elspeth went grimly out to challenge the forces of evil.

The woman was speaking to Debbie in a foreign accent.

"Can you be after tellin' me, my dearie, if a pretty red-haired lady has come hereabouts in the last little while?"

"Oh, you must mean Mistress Radcliffe, ma'am," said Debbie.

"Must I, then?" smiled the stranger encouragingly.

"If you mean the young widow—she's the prettiest red-haired lady I ever seen! She came here three weeks back and is living at Bennet Farm, between here and Elsinghurst," explained Debbie in a burst of words. "The one that's from America?"

The strange lady, putting back her veil, smiled broadly. "My own dear daughter! I have found her at last!" She raised her flat black beady eyes to the sky piously. "Heaven has heard a mother's prayers! Bless you, my child! You said she was in Elsinghurst, at the Bennet Farm?"

Elspeth could no longer resist the urge to meddle. She came out onto the wide inn porch and confronted the black-clad stranger. "You are claiming that Mistress Radcliffe is your daughter?"

The gaunt female, who certainly bore no resemblance to the red-headed temptress, fixed Elspeth with a glance at once fawning and vaguely threatening. "Sure an' we heard her young husband was killed in the Colonies, and it fair drove her mad with grief! The poor girleen ran away from her loving mother and all her good friends. 'Tis frantic we've been, trying to find her, for we feared she would do herself a mischief in her grief-stricken state. But I have that which will calm her mind and restore her happiness! Her own dear husband, not killed after all, but returned safely to her."

She pointed down the road, where a handsome youth trudged toward them from the direction of the other inn. "Asking for her all along the London road, we've been! I'll just run to tell Adrian that his poor wife is found!"

The black-clad woman hurried toward the man and they had a conference by the road. Then they both came toward the inn. Elspeth scrutinized them carefully. She was reluctant to abandon her conviction that Kathryn Radcliffe was a witch, whether or not she was Lady Nadine. Still, if she was crazed, and her mother and husband had come to take her back to London, that should serve almost as well. It would get rid of her. Elspeth realized that having Kathryn taken away out of all their lives was the thing she wanted most in the world. She neither liked nor trusted the newcomer, and the young man appeared to be no better than he should be—very flashy and bad-tempered he sounded, with his voice raised to his mother-in-law like a spoiled bairn. *But then,* thought Elspeth, with a surge of relief which quite surprised her by its intensity, *I don't have to live with any of them, and they will take that creature away from here!*

She resolved to help them all she could. "I'm Elspeth Cameron of Bennet Farm," she announced, approaching the arguing pair briskly. "Debbie has misinformed you. Your daughter's not at our farm. She's staying at the Reverend Archibald Percy's vicarage, over near Elsinghurst. You'd best jump right back on the coach and get over there to collect her."

Here her good luck received its first check. As she spoke, she observed with dismay that the London coach was drawing away from the George and Horse Inn.

"Hurry, then! You'll miss the coach!"

The young man sneered. "In that event, I'm sure you can lend us your broomstick!"

Elspeth whitened and drew back as from something evil. The woman tried to smooth things over. "You'll have to forgive a young husband, ma'am, half out of his senses with grief!" she began. But Elspeth was having no more to do with them. "'Tis my belief you're all witches and warlocks—you and that unholy creature you call daughter! I'm going to Father Percy this day, and tell him what a viper he has taken into his bosom!" She turned her back and hurried away to where she had stabled the cob.

Donner turned on Adrian Bart with a fury that shocked him. "I've let you come with me this far, little man, because I thought you'd be of some use to me in getting Nadine back to Ireland. I had that old bitch ready to help us and you wrecked all with your loose mouth. One more trick like that and I'll see you die."

Adrian tried to bluster, but his performance wasn't very convincing. He was afraid of this terrible old woman; he knew she would stop at nothing to achieve her purpose. Finally he capitulated.

"All right! So it was a mistake to taunt the old woman. What do we do now?"

"We hire a cart and we get over to Elsinghurst Village and spread it about that you're the husband reported dead in the Colonies. And we make very sure indeed that everyone believes Nadine is out of her mind with grief over the loss of you." She curled her lip scornfully. "Look pretty, little man, and very much the fine buck that sets the ladies' hearts to beating. If she denies us, or tries to run away again, we'll claim she's gone completely out of her mind, and we'll restrain her for her own good—poor mad girleen."

Adrian stared at her with loathing. "You devil!" he whispered.

Donner answered him with a harsh bark of laughter. "It's well for you that I am, little man! When we have her safe at Brionny Keep, I'll pay you your share of his fine lordship's money."

"And if she won't come with us willingly?"

"Then we'll compel her," said Donner with a quiet viciousness that silenced further protest.

Sixteen

While Donner and Adrian were dickering for a cart to carry them to Elsinghurst Village, Elspeth was already driving back to Bennet Farm at a pace which alarmed the sober old cob. In fact, he rebelled part way home, and neither voice nor whip could move him out of the stubborn walk he affected from then on. So it was that Elspeth arrived at the farm in a tight-lipped fury, to encounter Richard Bennet at the barns. Had she not been so angry, she might have been more circumspect. To his mild enquiry as to what errand had taken her from home, she snapped.

"I've been to Crofton discovering the truth about your precious Mistress Radcliffe. It seems she's no more a widow than I am, and her mother and husband are searching for her—" Elspeth faltered, alarmed at last by the expression on Richard Bennet's face. Normally the gentlest of men, he was staring at her with angry incredulity.

"You went to Crofton to make mischief for the girl? Is that what you are telling me?"

"She's no girl, Richard Bennet, as I have been forever telling you." Elspeth clung stoutly to her anger. "She's a married woman run off from her husband. I told them where to find her—"

"You meddler!" Richard's attack shocked Elspeth into momentary silence. "You had no business tattling! My sister trusted us to shelter the girl—"

"From her lawful husband?" snapped Elspeth, recovering her countenance.

"And who says he is her husband?" Richard challenged, his face unyielding.

At this evidence of male stupidity and bias, Elspeth's fragile control snapped. "Whoever he is, she's mixed up with him and that queer old woman. They're a precious pair of rascals. Birds of a feather flock together, as you ought to know. Decent folk are well rid of the lot of them. I couldn't find it in my conscience to remain under any roof where such persons were welcome," she concluded self-righteously.

"This is still my home, Elspeth Cameron," said Richard in a voice she had never heard him use, "and my orders must be obeyed. If you cannot find it in your conscience to accept my decisions, you must leave at once."

The woman stared into his face, unable to believe what she had heard. "You are telling me to go away from this farm, Richard? After the years I have worked here, faithfully, for you and your sister? After we have worked together—known each other?"

Richard considered her gravely. "It seems to me I

have never really known you until now." He turned away. "I'll saddle a horse and ride to the vicarage. If this is some trick, Kathryn may need help, and the Vicar is of no use in an emergency. Get the guest room ready for Mistress Radcliffe and Poll."

"You fool!" shrilled Elspeth. "You're besotted by her devil's face—!" but Richard had already left her.

Elspeth had never admitted to herself the depth and nature of her feeling for her employer, nor did she do so now. Instead she got into the trap again, and , seizing the whip, lashed the astonished cob into a reluctant trot. Her face was twisted in a scowl and she muttered to herself, "I'll save him from that witch ... I'll tell the villagers what sort of a viper they have nourished ... contaminating their children ... deceiving a besotted old man ..."

She was well on the way to Elsinghurst before Richard had saddled his horse. Unaware that Elspeth was launched on a mission of vengeance, he did not force the pace, but held his mount to a canter along the lane that was a short cut to Elsinghurst Village.

And at this very moment, Donner and Adrian were already at the Elsingham Arms in Elsinghurst, asking the way to the vicarage, and telling their story of the return from the dead of "the widow's" husband.

Seventeen

Quite unaware of the storm gathering in the village, Kathryn was pouring tea for the Vicar. They were seated in his pleasant parlor. The Reverend Percy beamed at the books so neatly arranged on the shelves, their white paper markers safely undisturbed. He eyed the flowers tastefully arranged and set out on dust-free tables, the fire burning cheerily in the fireplace, the curtains neatly drawn against the approaching night.

"It's a miracle. This house has never appeared so spacious, so inviting, yet every one of my books is where I can find it! In my study, too! You have worked the miracle, Kathryn."

"Thank the Dewey Decimal System," said Kathryn, handing him his cup and offering the toasted scones.

"I really shouldn't ... but so good with cheese and

jam." He busied himself with his plate, while Kathryn smiled fondly at him and poured her own tea. Speaking of miracles, she had never felt so useful, so needed, so fulfilled as since she came to the home of this gentle old man. They spoke the same language, she and the Reverend Archibald Percy.

"We're really misfits, you and I," Kathryn heard herself saying aloud. He lifted his white eyebrows in enquiry. "Not so much born out of time," she explained her comment, "as living outside the daily lives of our neighbors."

The Vicar gave this the same calm and careful consideration he gave to everything she said. It was one of his greatest charms, she thought. He was completely aware of her; he listened completely. The Reverend Archibald Percy, Kathryn had discovered, was vague only about material things. In the realm of ideas he was remarkably acute—"awake on all suits," as the current slang had it. His instant acceptance of her own amazing story had healed once and forever a festering wound of doubt in Kathryn's mind: that perhaps she was insane. It had not seemed impossible to this little cleric that a woman's soul might be transmitted from one century to another.

"The more we learn," he had said quietly, when she finished her strange story that first night, "the more we see there is to learn. You have spoken about the science and technology which, commonplace in your time, are to us in 1775 dazzling, challenging mysteries. Yet we ourselves accept as ordinary knowledge facts and ideas which would have terrified our ancestors. One must keep an open mind, and beware of self-righteous complacence."

Now again he was considering her words carefully.

"Yes, Kathryn, I am afraid I do live apart from the

daily concerns of my parishioners, both gentry and farmers. The world of abstract thought is not as attractive to them as it is to me. And so many of them have to struggle, dawn to dark, to earn enough to keep body and soul together, that they are too tired to enjoy anything but food and drink and sleep." He glanced at Kathryn. "And of course, sex." He smiled at her responsive chuckle, highly pleased that he had made her laugh.

"But you, my dear," he went on, "are far too young and beautiful to put yourself outside the stream of life. If you could only reconcile yourself to staying here—"

"To be exiled to a ruined castle in Ireland?" asked Kathryn. "In the power of a devilish woman who seems to have kept this body drugged and under her control? And who probably sent the soul of Nadine into the future for some evil purpose?"

The Reverend Percy stared at her, his mind busy. "But surely, with such beauty and knowledge as you possess, you could outwit some old peasant woman?"

"She has a power which frightens me," confessed Kathryn. "There is something about her which turns my spirit cold."

"From what I have heard you say of Lord John, he has behaved as a sensible and decent man. This agrees with my own limited personal experience with him. Perhaps together you and I might convince him that the wild, immature spirit of the Irish girl no longer inhabits this body—"

Kathryn stared at him, her face pale with shock. "Father Percy! Where is Nadine? If I am here in her body—"

His face brightened. "She must therefore be free of the dominance which might have destroyed her soul! You perceive, my dear child, that the workings of the

Deity, while inscrutable, are benevolent! You have given that poor immature being a chance to live and develop outside the influence of Donner."

"But if she is in my body ... she'll be *terrified!* The noise! The automobiles and subways—jet planes ..."

"We must commend her to God," said the Reverend Percy serenely. "Perhaps in that noisy, brawling, active city you have described, she will be more at home than you ever were."

"I hope she knows how to fight for what she wants," said Kathryn grimly. "I never learned how to." She winced as she recalled the scene on the bus and her feelings of humiliation. The Reverend Percy was watching her with surprisingly keen eyes. "I believe you will learn how now—when there is something you really want. I cannot believe your heart was set on that shallow and venial youth you described to me. Today we should call such a fellow an encroaching mushroom."

He was rewarded by a full-throated laugh from Kathryn. It was their special game to use slang from their respective eras. The priest was acquiring a colorful twentieth century vocabulary which Kathryn was afraid he would use inadvertenly some day to the confusion of his parishioners.

Diverted, Kathryn searched for the relevant expression. "In New York, we'd call his kind a sharpie—on the make—wheeling and dealing. I'm afraid Don was a social climber," she concluded. Suddenly a smile touched her lips and eyes. "Father Percy, I'm *free!* The thought of Don doesn't hurt any more."

The Vicar nodded encouragement. "That's a sensible girl! The fellow obviously isn't worth a thought!" He peered at her craftily. "And having made that decision, are you any closer to deciding to stay here and fight—"

He was interrupted by the hurried entrance of old Newton. "There's a lady here, sir, says she has to see Mrs. Radcliffe, only she calls her Mrs. Bart, and says she's her mother!"

Startled, Kathryn stared from Newton to his master. "Who can this be?" she whispered. "I know no Mrs. Bart."

"Oh, miss," quavered Newton. "It's the young man that's named Bart. Your husband, he claims. The old lady is called Mistress Donner."

Kathryn rose from her chair in a single convulsive movement.

"Donner! That's the woman who was drugging Nadine," she whispered in a panic. "She mustn't get in— I can't see her—"

The Vicar rose and moved to her side.

"Kathryn, my dear child, compose yourself! We'll confront her together. You are safe here under my roof. She cannot harm you unless you give her the power to do so by showing fear and weakness. Be calm."

Kathryn clung to his outstretched hand. "You don't know her! She is *evil*."

The Vicar took this calmly. "I have been aware of the existence of evil for many years. In fact you might say it has been my chief business to cope with it." He patted her hand. "Newton, you may show Mrs. Donner and Mr. Bart in."

"No!" protested Kathryn, and looked around her for a way of escape. How could this gentle, unworldly little man foresee the lengths to which a creature like Donner might go? "I won't see her—"

"Now is that any way to greet your own dear Ma, childeen?" Donner's voice came from the doorway. "'Tis my heart you'll be breakin' entirely." She came forward, her black dress and cape rustling. Kathryn had the image of a great bird of prey swooping. Donner hesitated, assessing the little white-haired man standing so quietly beside the girl. She seemed to dismiss the idea that he could be a threat to her, and advanced again toward Kathryn. Adrian Bart, all smiles, followed her into the room.

Kathryn caught at her courage with both hands. "Donner, you are not my mother. You know very well that I am not married to this artist—"

"Poor girleen!" sighed Donner, dabbing at her dry eyes with a grimy handkerchief. "Quite out of her mind again! It's not the first time," she confided to the Vicar. "She's had delusions and run away before. Sometimes she claims to be the Lady Nadine Elsingham, and othertimes she says she's a lost soul come here from the future. I hope I don't have to put the poor troubled creature into Bedlam!" She gave Kathryn a threatening glance.

Kathryn shrank back, white-faced.

Donner was quick to follow up this advantage. "Of course, if she's ready to come quietly with us who know and love her, we'll see she comes to no harm. Her poor husband, a saint if ever there was one," with a quick, admonitory glance at Bart, who was staring at Kathryn with a remarkably foolish expression on his face, "is more than willing to take her back and let me care for her quietly in our own home. Much pleasanter for the poor childeen than Bedlam, wouldn't you say, Your Reverence?"

The Vicar spoke at last. There was no shock or protest in his tone, merely an acceptance of human frailty.

"You are an evil woman, Mistress Donner. Kathryn told me about you. I had thought that perhaps she exaggerated, but you really are utterly without conscience. I have never met a human being without compunction before."

Donner stared at him, nonplussed. Her first quick scrutiny had classified him as a harmless old fool, frail and ineffectual, whom she could wheedle or bully as she pleased. Yet the words he had just spoken made her uneasy. He hadn't raised his namby-pamby, finicking old voice, with the cultured accent she envied while she scorned it, but he'd managed to frighten her more than many a younger man had been able to do. Still, she assured herself, he was nothing but a doddering old nincompoop. Surely she could bamboozle him easily enough! She adopted the tone of wheedling truculence she had used successfully to get her way with the Irish gentry.

"Now, then, Your Reverence, there's no need to be angry with old Donner! I'm sure we all want what's best for this poor, disturbed girleen—"

"Silence, woman!" commanded the Vicar, without heat but firmly. "I know what you are. You want nothing good for anyone. I warn you to cease your persecution of this woman. The soul you sought to entrap and degrade has escaped you by the Grace of God, and this soul has resources you cannot comprehend. For your own sake, woman, I charge you: leave us; return to your own place. *In Jesus' name.*"

He merely stretched out his arm, pointing to the door, but there was something in his voice and face which suggested an exorcism. The old man spoke as one commanding a demon.

Donner's lip drew back from her teeth in a grimace, half smile, half snarl; she turned, with one furious glance at Kathryn, and walked so quickly from the room that she caught Adrian Bart unprepared. He hurried out after her, embarrassed and resentful.

Newton, who had been hovering in the hallway, shamelessly eavesdropping, got the front door open in time, and watched with satisfaction as the two conspirators went down the walk, quarreling furiously.

Within the room, Kathryn was staring at the Vicar with respect. "You routed her! It was like an exorcism!"

The Vicar did not smile. "Kathryn, you did not exaggerate. That is a very evil spirit—arrogant and presumptuous. She hungers and thirsts for power—absolute power over other human beings. She dabbles in forbidden practices. There is the stink of witchcraft about her. And she is not defeated. She will return—reinforced. You must get away from this place at once."

"But where can I go? I can't return to Bennet Farm—"

"No, you must get completely out of her sphere of influence. She has controlled the body you now wear, so you will never be safe unless you can face her down yourself—"

"No, no!" Kathryn sobbed, and shook her head in fear.

"Then you must go where she cannot follow. Perhaps London—no! New York! She'd scarcely follow you there!"

While Kathryn was trying frantically to express her reluctance to go to the New York of 1775, Newton came spryly into the parlor, his eyes sparkling. Never in all his years with the Reverend Percy had so many interesting things happened.

"It's Farmer Bennet here now, sir, to see you and Mistress Radcliffe. He says it's urgent!"

"Show Mr. Bennet in at once, Newton. God grant it's not more trouble," the Vicar said to Kathryn.

As Richard entered the room, his eyes went at once to Kathryn's face. "Good evening, Kathryn," he said. "Thankee for seeing me, Father Percy," he went on. "I'm afraid I've brought rather bad news. Elspeth Cameron's gone daft. She came home from Crofton village full of some wild tale about meeting Kathryn's mother and—husband," he colored, then went on, quietly, "I felt I must warn you."

"The creature has been here already, and I have sent her and her attendant empty away," said the Vicar sternly. "However, I am convinced she will return. Kathryn must be gotten out of her reach at once. We were trying to think of a suitable place—"

"There's the farm," began Richard eagerly, and then shook his head. "Too close to hand. And Elspeth would never keep silent." He frowned with the effort of concentration. "Wait! I've had a message from Maggie. Just before Elspeth came storming in, a groom from the Manor rode over to tell me my sister had come to Elsinghurst and was very anxious to see me. So I think I should take Kathryn there at once."

"Yes, that would help. It won't do as a permanent sanctuary, for servants will talk, but it will get Kathryn out of Donner's ken for tonight. Your sister must help us to think of a safer place."

Kathryn had regained her color and her composure as she listened. "If Bennet is at the Manor, and has sent for me, that means she has the portrait there also. Don't you see it's the perfect refuge for me? I'll go back to my own time and place!"

The Vicar frowned. "My dear child, how can you hope to accomplish this? You were brought here, I truly believe, through some devilish sorcery of Donner's. Can you return without having recourse to similar practices?"

Kathryn stared at him, sick with disappointment. "I had thought I might just—look at the picture ... concentrate ... and return," she began miserably.

Richard, unable to bear the desolation on that beautiful face, came to stand beside her. "Let's get you safe to the Manor. I'll find a way to alert Maggie and we'll smuggle you in. It's such a great barn of a place there'll be many a room you could hide in for a month, and no one ever discover you."

Kathryn smiled up into his concerned face. "I'm lucky to have wonderful friends," she said softly. "I do agree with Father Percy that I should leave soon—"

"You're right about that, mistress," said Newton from the doorway. "There's a gaggle o' villagers coming up the road—some with torches—and they don't sound very friendly." He was holding Kathryn's cloak in his hands. With a smile and a word of thanks, Kathryn threw it over her shoulders and turned to the Vicar.

"We'll go out the kitchen door, Father Percy. If you can stall them off long enough for us to get away—"

"Go with Richard Bennet at once, my dear child." The Vicar was leading the way to the kitchen as he spoke. "Did you come by horseback, Richard?"

"He's in your stables, and he'll bear the extra weight gladly. There must be no horse missing to give them a clue."

"Go with God," said the Vicar fervently, and ran back into the house.

As Richard guided the great stallion down the narrow lane, he and Kathryn could see the flicker of torchlight through the trees, and hear the threatening gabble of voices approaching the front of the vicarage.

Eighteen

As *Richard* and Kathryn moved off through the woods toward Elsingham Manor, the Vicar was hastily briefing Newton.

"Hold them on the porch as long as you are able, Newton.. Then let just a few—the leaders—in to see me—"

"Nay, Vicar," protested the old servant shrewdly. "The ones left outside may go prowling about, seeking what they may devour, and we wouldn't want to give them a chance to get on Mistress's trail, would we?"

The Vicar was much struck by the wisdom of this. "Newton, old friend, you are a Machiavelli! What do you advise?"

Newton was already moving toward the front door. "Go back to your study, sir. I'll let them in the hall and come to get you," he said over his shoulder.

Already there was the sound of harsh voices and the trampling of feet on the broad porch of the vicarage. Someone pounded heavily on the brass knocker. A woman's voice called out the Vicar's name.

Newton approached the door with his usual unhurried gait. He opened it to reveal a mob of about fifteen persons, mostly women. At their head, obviously the leader, stood Elspeth Cameron. Newton, enjoying himself as never before, moved to the attack.

"Is the village burning down, then, Mistress Cameron? Or are you and these silly folk playing at All Fools' Eve? Your racket is enough to wake the dead."

"We'll see the Vicar, you doddering old skelpin," retorted Elspeth, but it was plain she was a little taken aback by the reception.

"Oh, you'll see the Vicar, will you, Elspeth Cameron?" Newton parodied her. "And all these brave gentlemen clinging to your skirts, will they see the Vicar, too? Is it arson and insurrection you're intending, Jonas Tilley? Going to burn down the vicarage with those torches? Is murder and revolution in the wind, Thomas Berry? Shall I call out the militia to defend the Vicar from his own parishioners?"

The men from the village were beginning to regret that they had let themselves be talked into this march. Faced with old Newton's mockery, they were discovering little stomach for a confrontation so unlike their usual, sober behavior. Jonas Tilley, the innkeeper, spoke in a moderated tone.

"'Twas Mistress Cameron telled us that young Mistress Radcliffe was a looney and a dissolute woman, run off from her lawful husband—"

"And where did Mistress Cameron discover these great truths?" wondered Newton. "I would have thought

182

that our innkeeper would be too busy to run tattling to the Vicar with women's gossip."

Elspeth Cameron had had enough.

"Stand aside, you old fool, and let us talk to the Vicar," she snapped, shouldering her way past Newton. The old man was a match for her. Ignoring her completely, he stepped in front of her again and directed his remarks to Jonas.

"So Bennet's housekeeper is doing your thinking for you now, Jonas?" he grinned. "Better you than me!"

Jonas glared at his tormentor resentfully. "Well, we thought it our duty to come and warn Vicar he was nourishing a viper in his house. My wife said—"

"So now it's your wife doing your thinking," commented Newton. "If it's not one woman it's another, telling you what to say."

There was a chuckle from the men in the crowd. Mrs. Tilley was well-known in the village.

Elspeth Cameron advanced on Newton, her face mottled with anger. "Step aside, you skelpin, or I'll—"

Reluctantly the Vicar decided it was time to interfere. He had been listening with pleasure to the utterances of his champion, but he knew enough about human nature to recognize the note of hysteria in Elspeth's voice. So he came placidly out into the hall, saying calmly, "Newton, who are these people making such a racket? Is there trouble in the village?"

"Trouble enough, Mr. Percy," shouted Elspeth. "We've come to warn you to get rid of that woman you're harboring—"

"Mrs. Cameron, is it?" asked the Vicar quietly. "My poor woman, are you ill? Do come in and sit down. How can I help you?"

"You old fool, it's yourself you'd better help—" began Elspeth. But this was too much for the men of the parish. Already embarrassed by the situation they had let themselves be led into by this woman, impressed as always by the Vicar's gentle dignity, they found themselves shocked and shamed by Elspeth's rudeness. And she not even a member of the church, but some non-conforming fanatic!

"Here, now then, Mistress Cameron, you'd best hold your tongue," advised Jonas sternly. And Mrs. Tilley, resentful though she was of Newton's behavior, was forced to agree with her husband that Farmer Bennet's housekeeper had no business calling the Vicar an old fool. She moved forward and took Elspeth's arm.

"Come away, Mrs. Cameron. We'll let the men handle it," she suggested gently enough, but her words and gesture angered Elspeth beyond endurance. To think that the girl she hated should be resting peacefully within this house, protected by the Vicar from getting her just deserts, and that now the village folk she had roused against the creature were turning craven ... they'd let the wanton stay here to corrupt the hearts and minds of decent men like Richard Bennet, stupid fool that he was, too blind to see what the woman really was ... ! Elspeth could not endure it. She jerked her arm out of Mrs. Tilley's grasp and lunged toward the Vicar.

"You are harboring that Jezebel! Separating husband and wife! What kind of immorality is this in a Christian household?"

The Vicar did not flinch under the wild attack. "Poor woman, she is beside herself. Here, Tilley, Barry, help her into the parlor and I'll have Newton prepare a cup of tea for her. Some of you ladies come in too; this poor creature cannot be left unattended. Is she having a fit, do you think? Should one of you men go for the doctor?"

Elspeth, firm in the grasp of the two men, stared from the Vicar's gentle face to the stern visages of her captors. Then she glared around at the rest of her following, now a very sheepish-looking mob indeed. She knew she had lost the battle.

"No need for that," she managed to say, harsh-voiced. "I'll return to Bennet Farm, since these timorous Sassenachs have no stomach for a battle against evil. But I warn you all," and she glared around the circle, "you'll rue this night's work, when that wanton destroys your children and ensnares your men—"

Whatever else she might have said was cut off as the villagers, uneasy now at the situation they had created, hustled her out of the Vicar's hallway and onto the porch. Remembering that Richard Bennet would not be at the farm, the Vicar called out, "One moment, please, Tilley! I cannot bear to think of that poor woman trying to make her way home alone to the Bennet Farm. I suggest, therefore, that your good wife put her up in a room at your inn—I shall pay the charges, of course. Then she can have a quiet night to recover her wits before she takes the drive to the farm."

There was a general murmur of approbation at this generous forbearance on the part of the offended party, and several men were heard to tell their wives that THAT was the man they had been urging their husbands to attack, and how they'd be able to face the good Vicar on Sunday their husbands couldn't imagine. Whereat several of the wives protested that it wasn't *their* idea to come on this wild-goose chase, and of course everyone knew the Vicar was a saint.

Listening to these and other comments as the erstwhile mob wended its way cautiously down the driveway and along the road—for the torches, neglected, had long gone out—the Vicar closed his door with relief. And turned to find Newton at his elbow with two large glasses filled to the brim.

Silently the Vicar accepted one, and silently master and servant toasted one another's performance.

Nineteen

Richard was sorry that the distance between the vicarage and the Manor was so short. He had never held a woman as he now held Kathryn, seated before him on the saddle. She was warm and soft, yet firm, and he was very conscious of her fragrance and resilience in his arms.

"I am in love," he said quietly, and felt her sudden tenseness.

Her magnificent eyes gleamed up at him in the dark of the woods. "I am not free," she said at length. Her voice was soft.

"You are—Lady Nadine?" It was Richard's turn to stiffen. His arm, supporting her, became iron-hard.

"No, truly I am not," said Kathryn. "I cannot explain, but I do have a connection with that unhappy girl. And I am in great danger."

"From Elspeth?" asked Richard, his voice rough with anger. "I'll send that meddler packing tomorrow!"

"Not on my account—please. Donner and her companion are a far greater threat to me. And to others! Donner must not find me."

"Maggie can keep you safe," muttered Richard. It was obvious that running and hiding were two activities Richard Bennet had no sympathy with, yet he respected Kathryn's feelings and would make no move she had not sanctioned. The big quiet fellow was finding his first love a painful business, but he was too much a man to impose his emotions on the woman he loved. Kathryn, sensing his effort at control, was anxious to change the subject.

"Where are we to meet your sister?"

"I'll stow you safe in the Manor park, in a little Grecian summerhouse that's seldom visited, while I seek out Maggie. She'll have thought of a way of smuggling you into the Manor and hiding you."

Kathryn waited in the summerhouse, a tiny enchanted place of tall silver-white columns and pale marble floors. She had thought she would be more nervous of snakes and spiders than of discovery, but the little archaic temple imposed its own peace on her frightened spirit. In a very short time, Richard returned with his sister. Bennet hugged the girl with motherly affection. Kathryn found herself crying. Richard grinned at them both.

"Best save the tears and gossip till we have you safely bestowed," he advised. Bennet became her competent self at once.

"You've done your part well, Richard. Back to the farm with you now, so there'll be no way to connect our guest Kathryn Radcliffe with the Manor," she said briskly.

"Thank you, Richard." Kathryn held out her hand. "You've been my shield and buckler."

Richard kissed her hand with simple courtliness. Unable to trust his voice, he waved at his sister and slipped away in the dark.

Bennet led the girl through a series of gardens—formal, herb, and kitchen—past beds of sweet-smelling flowers and under blossoming fruit trees. For a few minutes there was the acrid pungence of ivy as they moved along a path beside a high wall. Then the great bulk of the Manor loomed up in front of them. A few lights showed in the windows to the rear of the house, but for the most part the beautiful old building was dark.

"Quietly now," whispered Bennet, leading the way to a small door concealed in flowering shrubs. She opened it soundlessly, and took Kathryn's hand to guide her. There was a small staircase up which they moved in silence, and finally a heavy old door which creaked alarmingly in spite of Bennet's caution. Once the door was closed behind them, the older woman panted a sigh of relief. "We're in the attics, now, Miss Kathryn. No one ever comes up here since her ladyship died. It's used for storage. I can make you comfortable enough here until we can get you down to see the portrait."

"You got it here! Oh, Bennet, thank you! When can we—?"

"Not tonight, Miss Kathryn," said Bennet firmly. "You've been through enough. Richard told me a little of it when he was bringing me to you. No, tonight you will rest and regain your strength." She opened the door proudly to show a small room where a lamp glowed softly.

Kathryn exclaimed with pleasure.

It was a child's playroom, or had been at one time. A spirited rocking horse cocked a wise dark eye from the corner where he stood guard over a neat cot, freshly made up with crisp white sheets and pillows. On the small round table there was the lamp, a plate with a crusty loaf of bread, a covered dish of cheese, and a bottle of wine.

Kathryn turned to meet Bennet's smiling look. Laughing and crying at the same time, she threw her arms around the older woman. "Dear Bennet! What would I ever have done without you? This is like a fairy tale!"

"It was Master John's secret room," confided Bennet. "Only he and I knew of it. He used to come up here when he was in a temper, or had been hurt . . . and he said the room helped him." Her eyes were tender. "He was a fine boy, Miss Kathryn, and he's grown into a good man. I do believe he'll help you if you let him—"

But Kathryn had drawn away. Her eyes lost their warmth as she said, quietly, "Have you forgotten that he ordered me to go to Ireland? You know what that would mean, especially since Donner has found me again. Bennet, I could not bear it. I'll—I'll die first!"

"Let me hear no more of that foolish talk, Miss Kathryn," said Bennet sternly. "You're tired and overwrought with all the trouble, and small wonder. Get a good night's sleep, now. I'll slip up in the morning to bring you hot tea. Just don't make any noise, Miss Kathryn." Bennet took a last look at the arrangements she had made for the girl's comfort, then, giving her a pat on the shoulder, she went softly away.

Washing her face at the tiny commode and drying her hands on a soft towel, Kathryn wearily made ready for bed. There was so much to think about, so much to plan, that she felt dull and confused. Sighing, she blew out the lamp and got thankfully into the cot. In a few minutes, in spite of her determination to 'think things out,' she was asleep.

She awoke with good appetite and ate some of the delicious country bread and cheese before she even dressed. The wine she reserved for a later time, but some water in a covered jug was ample to slake her thirst. Then, leisurely, she dressed and examined her surroundings. This was John's room, his childhood sanctuary. Strange that it should be hers now, should shelter her from the man whom that boy had become. Oh, Kathryn thought wistfully, if I had known him then! If we had been friends as children! *Or were now,* her treacherous heart suggested. How blind, how stupid, Nadine was to deceive this man and reject what he had to offer a woman! She caught the bright eye of the great rocking horse and felt herself blushing.

So. Admit it, Kathryn. You are in love with a man who fears and hates the things you seem to be. Who could never completely trust you and surely never truly love you while you wear this flesh. She straightened her shoulders and faced the bright, too-knowing eye.

"I'll leave as soon as I can get safely down to the portrait," she told that eye firmly.

"And if the business with the portrait doesn't work?" the bright eye challenged.

"It must. It worked once," Kathryn argued.

"But if it doesn't?"

Kathryn wasn't sure whether she was arguing with a rocking horse or with herself. "If it doesn't work, then I'll go away to some city where no one ever heard of the Elsinghams, and I'll find a job and live out my life as best I can," she promised herself. And felt better.

She had the bed made, the room tidied, and was

looking through a dog-eared book of Master John's when Bennet came into the room.

"Good morning, my dear," she said softly, scanning Kathryn's face carefully. Apparently satisfied with what she saw, she closed the door quietly and placed a steaming pot of tea upon the table. Pouring Kathryn a cup, Bennet said, "We'll have to remember to keep our voices down to a whisper. Mustn't let any of the upstairs maids suspect there's a guest in the attic!"

"This," said Kathryn, sipping the hot sweet brew greedily, "is ambrosia—mead...what does mead really taste like, Bennet? Have you tasted it?"

Bennet smiled indulgently. "Now Miss Kathryn, is it likely I'd be carousing with such a heathen drink? Wassailing, I suppose you'd have to call it." Then relenting, she smiled. "It's sweet, you naughty child. Made from fermented honey...You don't look any older than Master John, when he was up to his mischief in this very room."

The reference to Lord John took the smile off Kathryn's face. "When can we go to the portrait, Bennet? Where have you placed it?"

"I've had it hung in the Great Hall, above the fireplace," whispered Bennet. "It's directly opposite the entrance doors, just as it was facing the front door in the London house. It—it *feels right* there, Miss Kathryn. It dominates the hall just as it did the one in London. The eyes—" the older woman hesitated. "They're strange...sort of hungry, and waiting..."

Kathryn felt a cold prickling over her skin. Putting its warning aside, she said, "Of course they're strange. They have the secret of pulling me back to my own world. I'm glad they are—waiting."

Bennet was deeply uneasy. She knew she must not weaken the girl's resolution at this crucial time, but the hazards appalled the simple, God-fearing woman. What if this lovely girl ended up in some other *place*—neither her own home nor Lady Nadine's? "Well, Miss Kathryn," she made herself say calmly, "you know what is best for yourself, I suppose, but—" she broke off, and her eyes misted with tears. "Oh, Miss Kathryn, I wish you could find it in your heart to stay here and fight it through! You're so much better for Master John than that Nadine!"

Kathryn hardened her will. "Lord John doesn't want either of us," she said harshly. "And I cannot say I blame him. We've both been nothing but trouble. Now, let's be sensible and plan when I'm to face the portrait."

Bennet sighed and nodded. "If your mind is made up, tonight's as good as any time. The longer we wait—"

"The more chance there is we'll be interrupted," agreed Kathryn.

"We've got none of that stuff Donner gave her ladyship," warned Bennet, "but I did bring the dress. It's been mended so it looks just as it did when—that is, that afternoon—"

"Thank you. You've been my real friend, Margaret Bennet. I'll never forget you."

Bennet's practical Scot's commonsense came to their rescue in time to prevent a tearful scene. "Let's not rejoice too soon, Miss Kathryn. It may be the portrait won't work without that creature Donner and her drugs ... And I'd be just as happy if it didn't," she murmured under her breath. "Happier."

Kathryn thought it wiser not to ask the older woman to repeat what she had said. She would not let herself admit it, but these weeks of challenge and fear and bittersweet happiness were the most exciting and fulfilling ones in her whole life. It had been a sterile, lonely life, she knew now, being always the outsider looking in at other people's shared family fun and interests and concerns. Being no one's choice, no one's beloved—not even Don's, really. For he had wanted the connection with the Hendrix name, the prestige the other branch of Kathryn's family enjoyed. *Never really me,* she thought, but without the pang of grief she had felt in the past. She was cured of Don, and it hadn't been all that hard. It will be harder, she told herself, to cure yourself of a tall, golden-haired Englishman with eyes that could be warm and tender or ice-gray and challenging. Life, she thought wistfully, would never be dull with a man like Lord John.

Bennet returned later in the morning with the garish golden dress and draped it over the rocking horse.

"Try to rest awhile, Miss Kathryn," she advised. "I'll slip back to help you into it after midnight, and then we'll try—"

"Yes," Kathryn said, and a shiver of—fear, was it?—rippled over her skin. "Tonight, we'll try!"

Twenty

Donner and Adrian Bart were eating dinner in the public room of the Elsingham Arms, Proprietor Jonas Tilley. They were being served by a tight-lipped Mistress Tilley, who had not yet come to terms with what had happened the night before at the vicarage. What with feeling anger at Elspeth Cameron for leading them all on a wild-goose chase, and shame that the Vicar had seen her in such raggletail company, Martha Tilley could not find an attitude to take which would give her exacerbated feelings any comfort. She was paying little attention to the rather unprepossessing guests she was serving until something the young man said startled her.

His voice was loud and his accent, Mistress Tilley thought, extremely common. "Are you sure it was really Nadine?"

The older woman hissed something at him and glanced warily around the room. Martha pretended to be very busy slicing the ham on the sideboard. The man muttered resentfully, "Who needs to be wary of these country bumpkins?"

The woman whispered something, and Bart's voice rose.

"Of course I checked the stages! There were two in this metropolis—one, going south, the other, north. Nadine wasn't on either of them."

'Nadine!' Martha Tilley's mind buzzed with conjecture. Rumors had filtered down from the servants at the Manor. As eighth generation tenants of the Elsingham estates, no villager was ignorant of the escapades of his lordship's Irish wife. Could it be—?

Martha nodded her head decisively, left the room and sent the kitchen maid to serve the two guests in the public room. She threw a shawl over her shoulders, for once careless of her appearance in public, and hastened down the back lane to the cottage of Mistress Latchet, who had worked with the mysterious stranger in the vicarage. And had, thought Martha Tilley, resentfully, as good as sponsored her. All that talk about a dame's school for their children! Maybe Elspeth Cameron was in the right of it! Martha, finding at last a satisfactory scapegoat for her own uncomfortable feelings, stepped out briskly for the house of a woman she had never really liked.

Within half an hour she was back at the inn in company with a very disturbed Mistress Latchet. They were arguing as they entered the public room. Donner and Bart were still at the table, talking low-voiced. Martha Tilley marched up to their table.

"Are you the woman who has been seeking her

196

daughter at Bennet Farm?" she asked abruptly.

Donner's flat black eyes swiveled up at her. After a minute she smiled widely. "I can see you have found out my secret. I should have known a woman as wise as yourself, ma'am, could see through my little stratagem!"

Soothing words indeed to ruffled sensibilities! Had Martha Tilley been less angry and less ashamed, she might have noticed that this common woman had not answered her question, nor had she given any information, just flattery. Martha, scenting exoneration, pursued the matter grimly.

"This is Mistress Latchet, who has worked with the stranger at the vicarage. She says the woman is highly educated, dines every night with Vicar, talking to him in his own language. Like Quality." Her eyes made disparaging comment on the lack of that commodity apparent in her customers. She drew an angry breath. "The woman claims she is a Mistress Radcliffe, a widow. You claim she is your daughter. But you spoke of her as *Nadine*."

Donner's smile was as wide as a wolf's. "You are too clever for us, ma'am! I see we can no longer deceive you. But I must pray your indulgence for a poor madwoman—"

"'Madwoman'!" The two good ladies echoed this dreadful word. Flushed with satisfaction, Mistress Tilley demanded, "Is she then Lady Nadine Elsingham, and not your daughter?"

Donner put on a manner in which admiration and sorrow were skilfully blended. "You've found out our dreadful secret! I only hope you keep silent for his lordship's sake."

"You said—a madwoman?" faltered poor Mistress Latchet. Then she rallied. "I can't—I don't believe you!

197

So kind, so pleasant and lively she was—always friendly and well-spoken."

Donner shook her head mournfully. "Aye, she's Quality-trained, whatever she's become. That's the tragedy of it—and she little more than a girl. Ah, there's black blood in the Brionnys, and dark things done in the old castle keep!"

The two women, birds to a snake, drew closer in horrified fascination. "—Dark things?" prompted Martha Tilley avidly.

Donner sighed. "His lordship was completely deceived. We in the village could have warned him, knowing the ugly history of her family, but fear of her spells kept us silent, alas!"

Adrian was staring at her with the same fascination the women showed. She was a devil's daughter, with her smooth tongue and her fertile imagination. Donner's flat black gaze was holding them all. She licked her lips.

"Sure an' his lordship soon learned what he had wedded, but the dear man had mercy, and tried to send her quietly back to her father. In my care, she was, as she had been since a child. I," announced Donner unctuously, "being the only one who could control her when she was in one of her murderous fits."

"'Fits'!" chorused the two women.

"Oh, it's terrible, terrible! The poor girleen goes quite mad at the change of the moon!"

Doing it rather too brown, thought Adrian. Mrs. Latchet appeared to agree with him.

"I don't believe you!" she said, weakly.

Martha Tilley snapped at her. "We've none of us known her for as long as a month. How do you know what's to do when the moon changes?"

"But that's not the worst." Donner was warming to

her work. "I've been given the drugs to calm her down—from her doctor in Ireland," she hastened to add. "It's when she's this way—clear in her mind like now—that she's most dangerous." She paused. Three pairs of eyes were fixed, hypnotized, on hers. Donner delivered her clinching thrust. "When she's like this, she practices witchcraft!"

The women cried out in fear. Martha turned on Mistress Latchet. "There's the woman you wanted to have teach the children! A fine coven of young witches and warlocks we'd have, if we let that creature loose on them!"

Mrs. Latchet began to cry.

Donner spoke soothingly. "No harm's done yet, ma'am, for I'm here with this strong young man to take her safe back to Ireland, and no one—child or adult—a penny the worse for it, *if we get her away quick and quiet!*" she added darkly.

"I'll call the constable—" began Martha Tilley self-righteously.

"I'm sure Your Honor's good sense and kindness will prevail," interrupted Donner hastily. "We none of us want to bring any more trouble on Lord Elsingham, do we, now? Just take me to the poor creature and Mr. Bart and I will do what is needful." She looked encouragingly at Martha Tilley.

That dame snorted angrily. "She's sought sanctuary with the Vicar. The old man's besotted with her."

"Oh, no! The poor old man! He is the first victim of her evil spells. Now if some few of us could go quietly and take her away before she does more harm—"

"She isn't there any longer," announced Mistress Latchet, wiping her eyes. "Polly Bradley, who's been her abigail, went home to her father's farm this morning. She stopped by to see me. Crying she was, because her dear Mistress Radcliffe had gone away in the night."

"Gone away!" Donner's face was ugly with disappointment. "Does no one know where she is, then?"

Martha Tilley narrowed her eyes and pursed her lips. "If she hasn't left the neighborhood—and the young man said he'd watched who got on both stage-coaches—then there's one place left where she may be..."

"Where?" Donner controlled her impatience.

"At the Manor. If she's Lady Nadine, that's her own place, isn't it?"

"Is Bennet there?" demanded Donner.

"Yes, she is. She got here two nights ago, on the late coach."

"Then Nadine is there, in hiding!" announced Donner. "For, much though I hate to tell you this, ma'am, but I guess such a clever woman as yourself will soon figure it out, Nadine has had Bennet in her power for weeks. It was them practicing witchcraft in Lord John's London house that started the whole thing. He caught them, Lady Nadine and Bennet, casting a spell in front of the new portrait."

"The portrait!" gasped Martha. "But that came down last week from London, and one of the gardeners told us he helped a footman to hang it yesterday at Mistress Bennet's orders!"

"God ha' mercy!" ejaculated Donner, putting on a wide-eyed expression. "Then there's no time to be lost, indeed. 'Tis certain they'll be at their wicked deeds this very night!"

"What shall we do?" faltered Martha. The whole thing was getting too alarming. "The Manor—his lordship—we can't just break into the *Manor*—!"

Donner kept herself under tight control. "True, true,

dear clever woman that you are! You've put your finger on it. We can't break in, but I am Lady Nadine's nurse and keeper, and his lordship has instructed me to convey her safely to Ireland, where the poor soul may have treatment in peace and quiet. And his lordship's not at the Manor. He's still in London."

This latter intelligence removed most of Martha's qualms.

Donner pursued her advantage. "Now you being such a sensible woman, and a leader in the village, as anyone can plainly see, will help me explain the problem to the men, and we'll all go peacefully and find the poor mad girl. I have her medicine here—" she patted her leather reticule, "and as soon as she has it, she'll come quiet as a lamb."

Martha Tilley was remembering last night's fiasco. "Perhaps it would be better, ma'am, if you was to go alone."

Donner, still holding her smile, shook her head. "Bennet's no better than her slave, and will do whatever the witch tells her. I may need help to get the medicine into her before she casts a spell on more honest folk. Like she has on little Polly," Donner added, looking at Mistress Latchet.

That good woman's face hardened. "Nothing must hurt Poll," she said fiercely. "She's like my own child, and her mother my best friend!"

"Then we'd better get the witch away," advised Donner sternly, "or there's no saying what dreadful things she'll make innocent folk do. She's already bewitched the Vicar and Bennet and Poll, that we know of."

This was more than enough for the two women. Lady Nadine's name was notorious, even in this small village so far from London, and the women were ready to believe the worst of 'Kathryn Radcliffe,' when they learned who she really was. They hurried off to get reinforcements, urging Donner to wait for them. She agreed, and when the two dames were out of earshot, she began to laugh.

"You devil!" said Adrian Bart, between admiration and revulsion. "Take care they don't burn her at the stake!"

"Better that than having her escape me," said Donner. She had ceased to laugh. She would never confide in any other human being, but there was something about this new Nadine which challenged and intimidated her, yet offered certain dazzling possibilities. What *had* happened, that night in Lord John's town house? Had she really extended her powers through time and space? Donner's lust for dominion raged like a fire. She had to regain control of whatever it was in Nadine's body, and bend and break it to her, Donner's, will.

Twenty-One

Just about this time, on the London road not twenty miles from Elsinghurst Village, a luxurious vehicle was halted by the roadside. Lord John Elsingham's coachman, impressed by his master's request that he 'put 'em along,' had cut one turn rather narrow. Unfortunately the driver of the London Mail, who was aware that he was eleven minutes behind his time, was springing his own horseflesh, and swept around the same turn a shade wide. Quick reactions and superb skill on the part of both drivers had averted a crash, but Lord John's coach had ended up with two wheels in the ditch. A worse thing was discovered when Lord John's coachman and the groom clambered down to lead the horses out of the ditch. One of the magnificent animals had a bad sprain and would have to be led to the nearest inn.

Lord John took the check calmly, reassuring his servants and speaking gently to his cattle, but his friends exchanged worried glances. They had not sat in the coach with him for several hours without realizing that Lord John's nerves were on the stretch. He had never been a moody or notional man, so his urgent desire to get to the Manor, and his sense of trouble approaching, impressed them more than they wished to admit. When the horses were unharnessed and led out of the ditch, the groom offered to mount one and ride back to the last inn they had passed to get a fresh team.

"Why don't you let Olson lead the lame horse instead," Lord Peter suggested. "It's only a mile or so. We'll wait here, Johnny, and you can ride ahead on a sound horse."

"Are you mad?" interposed Randall. "He's got no saddle, for one thing—"

"Do it, Johnny," urged Lord Peter.

Troubled blue eyes met steady gray ones for a long moment.

"You feel it too?" asked Lord John.

"No," admitted Lord Peter honestly, "but I feel you feeling it."

Lord John laughed without mirth. "I'll do it."

When they had seen their friend off, Randall turned to Lord Peter. "Now perhaps you'll have the kindness to explain what that was all about?"

Lord Peter frowned. "Johnny's convinced that his wife is in immediate danger."

Randall delivered himself of a series of colorful oaths, to which the coachman, standing by the carriage, listened with pleasure. Now that has some style to it, he thought, wishing his own master had a little of Mr. Towne's fluency. A real education to listen to, was Mr. Towne.

Lord Peter was neither amused nor edified. "When you can control your mouth," he said icily, "perhaps you will be good enough to explain what is annoying you."

Randall stared at him incredulously. "'*Annoying*'? You mean you don't know? 'I feel you feeling it,' was, I believe, the phrase you used. I might have expected to hear a speech like that from my Great-aunt Dolcina, who is as mad as a March hare, but from the lips of a man whose wits I had always rated as adequate, if not brilliant—!"

"Take a damper," advised his friend. "There's something devilish odd about this whole business—"

"Now there," interrupted Randall cordially. "You cut close to the bone. I reject 'annoying,' and when you describe your 'feelings' my gorge rises, but I most heartily endorse both 'devilish' and 'odd'—odd for you and Johnny, and devilish for Nadine."

"That's just it, you idiot. Johnny really believes she's changed—and so do I."

And while his friend glared at him open-mouthed, Lord Peter strolled over to engage the coachman in desultory conversation.

Twenty-Two

Kathryn had passed the day very quietly in the attic room. Since she was so soon to leave this time and place, she felt it important that she experience as much, as fully, as she was able. She even pulled aside one of the heavy red rep curtains which covered the dormer windows, and stared through the narrow space at a part of the Manor grounds. From this angle, she could not see the extensive gardens through which Bennet had led her the night before. The view from this window was of green velvet lawns sloping down to a little lake, in the middle of which floated a tiny island. The whole landscape was so exquisite that Kathryn found herself smiling and wishing very much that she could go down and walk in it. On the green lawns were a few noble old trees which cast a gracious shade.

"I'll remember this," Kathryn told herself, and had a sudden unpleasant memory of Central Park, with its noisy crowds, dust, litter and threat of muggers. The serene lawns and noble trees of the Manor took on a glamor and glow of venerable sweetness, a sort of innocence which reminded Kathryn of the Vicar.

The Vicar—Newton—Polly—Mrs. Latchet—Margaret and Richard Bennet...suddenly Kathryn's eyes were brimming with tears, and she felt an almost unbearable wave of homesickness—for this century she was to leave. She blinked away the tears angrily. How foolish can you get? she mocked herself. You haven't known these people for a month—the Vicar just over a week—and you're lonely for them already! When you get back to New York you'll forget about them, she promised herself.

Liar!

With a sob, Kathryn twitched the curtain shut and went to sit on the narrow cot. Admit it, she thought, you love them all. John and the Vicar and Bennet and Richard...even little Poll, and you're doing your darnedest to get away from them. She cried for a while, and then she dried her eyes resolutely and got up to prepare for the encounter with the portrait.

"Get with it," she advised herself, deliberately crude, "unless you want to be shoved in the looney bin or locked up in some creepy castle dungeon for the rest of your life. Little old New York is better, even with the noise and smog and dirt."

She brushed the beautiful hair and back-combed it into a high, elaborate coiffure, as close as she could get to the shape she remembered in the picture. She was quite unaware that far below her a stammering gardener's helper had confided a frightening experience to the head gardener, who had boxed his ears and then gone to the kitchen to relate the story to the cook, who had given him a mug of beer and requested him to tell it again to a breathless group of kitchen maids and footmen.

"A white, ghastly face it was," said the head gardener, making the most of his moment, "peering out of one of the attic windows and beck'nin'."

Beck'nin'?" breathed a maid in horrified delight. "To *him?*"

"Beck'nin'," repeated the head gardener firmly. "To whoever would come."

A shiver of fear went through his audience. To think! A ghost in the very attics above them! And *beck'nin'!* Two housemaids began to get hysterical, one vowing she could *never sleep another night* under this roof.

Cook realized she must nip this in the bud, or have a gaggle of silly fools vying with one another to establish who had the most sensitive nerves.

"Well, if that's the way you feel, Sookie, you may stay awake and scrub the scullery and kitchen floors. *And* polish the spoons. And if you still can't sleep after that, I'll lay out some ironing for you to do."

This Spartan treatment effectively cured the incipient hysterics, but it also ended the head gardener's hour of triumph. He finished his beer and tramped off to his tiny cottage, muttering to himself about silly females who couldn't take a joke. And he'd rather have a dozen of ghosts any day, than one old spoilsport besom.

But when she had successfully cowed the staff and got them back at their respective duties, the cook went quietly upstairs to tell the butler, Mr. Ponty, what the boy had seen. He in turn told Mrs. Bennet—and she encouraged him in his supercilious laughter.

"Believe me, Mrs. Bennet, they are a pack of credulous farmers, and Cook is no better than the rest of them," he said. He fought a running battle with Cook, who had been at the Manor longer than he had. "Ghosts in the attics, indeed! It'll be bats in the belfry next for Cook and her cohorts," said Ponty, and was rewarded by almost hysterical laughter from Bennet.

It was unfortunate that Bennet, using a headache as an excuse, left the servants' hall early and crept upstairs to the attics. She missed the stealthy arrival of a determined group of villagers led by Donner. They had learned from the fiasco of the night before, and instead of storming the Manor with shouts and flaring torches, they came quietly to the kitchen door and asked in a seemly fashion for an audience with Mr. Ponty. That worthy, anxious to reestablish ascendancy over Cook, was more willing than he might normally have been to listen to their strange tale.

Unaware of this, Bennet was in Lord John's playroom helping Kathryn to don the orange satin gown. "It's as well you are leaving tonight," she admitted. "The gardener's youngest helper saw you at the window this afternoon and thought you were a ghost. It's put all the servants into an uproar."

Kathryn began to explain and apologize, but Bennet brushed that aside. "It is rather fortunate than the reverse," she decided. "Now not a blessed one of them will venture to put his nose outside a bedroom door till it's daylight." She stood back to check Kathryn's appearance. "Perfect! We can go down soon. They'll all be hurrying off to bed, none of them anxious to be the last one left in the dark."

She stood by the round table, looking at Kathryn. She had never been close to Lady Nadine, scarcely even spoken to her. But she had glimpsed her from a distance, and it seemed to Bennet that the beautiful face, now white and tired, was more exquisite than it had ever been. Something about the eyes, Bennet thought. A shadow of pain bravely accepted, a flash of good humor, a softness of compassion, made the beautiful green eyes tender, and disciplined the whole face into lovely maturity.

"Oh, Master John," thought Bennet, "why aren't you here to see what your lady has become?" Even in the garish gown, Kathryn-Nadine was a triumphantly beautiful woman.

Kathryn smiled encouragingly at her. "Well, Bennet? Shall we try a little white magic?"

Bennet shuddered involuntarily. God forgive me, she prayed, I'm still hoping it won't work! And yet she knew that the alternatives: confinement in Bedlam or in the ruined Irish castle—were worse. Sighing, she took up the lamp and led the way down the stairs to the Great Hall.

When they reached the floor above the Great Hall, they became aware of a murmur of voices. They drew back, alarmed, and Bennet blew out her lamp.

Lights flared up in the Hall. Led by Ponty, what seemed like the whole staff of servants came into sight. Nearly every one carried a candle or a lamp. A footman went quickly from one wall sconce to the next, and in a few seconds the Great Hall was aglare with light. The portrait she had come deviously to confront blazed in the harsh light, a focus of color dominating the Hall. It was so close she could read the arrogance on that beautiful face—yet it was separated from her by her enemies. For, as she hid in the shadows, Kathryn perceived with a shock of fear that Donner and Adrian Bart were standing beside Ponty.

The butler began to direct his staff and the villagers. "Four of you men will stay here in case the witch should try to escape through the front door. Stop Mrs. Bennet if you see her. Place her under restraint if necessary; it is for her own good. The rest of you will accompany me and Donner, as we go from room to room, searching for the Lady Nadine."

"What if she flies out a window?" called a man's voice, obviously more than half serious. Ponty ignored the question.

"The gardeners and grooms are posted outside, all around the house. There's four men in the kitchen. If the lady is in this house, she will not escape us."

"She's here!" Donner's nostrils flared with a fine dramatic flourish. "I can sense the taint of witchcraft! Can ye not smell the brimstone?"

There were cries and groans from the women servants.

Hidden in the shadows above them, Kathryn listened incredulously. This was a witch-hunt! Did Donner mean to have her killed? And how had Donner found her so quickly?

At this moment, startling both the hunters and the hunted into shocked immobility, there sounded the heavy booming of the iron knocker on the panel of the great oaken door. The butler, conditioned by a lifetime of training, was the first to recover. Catching the eyes of two footmen, he began a stately advance toward the door.

Donner, with a mixture of avidity and alarm on her face, caught at his arm. "It's some trick of the witch! Don't open that door! Mayhap it's the Devil himself!"

The maids squealed in terror, but Ponty, ignoring Donner's clutch, continued his stately movement to the front door.

"Permit me to know my duty, ma'am," he told Donner coldly. *Common trash,* his supercilious dismissal said.

212

Donner gave him her snarling wolf-smile. She twisted her hands. *So close! Nothing must stop me now!*

The knocking was repeated, thunderously.

Ponty opened the door.

On the threshold, a towering figure of anger, stood the master of Elsingham Manor.

"You keep me waiting, Ponty," he said icily.

At once the hall was a reverberation of voices: the villagers, the servants, the butler, all hastening to explain the unexplainable, defend the indefensible. Donner had faded to the rear of the group, waiting in the shadows for her dupes to provide an opportunity for her, but meanwhile quite content to let them face the challenges and the punishment.

Milord did not even need to lift his hand to silence the babel. His attitude was enough. When the great room was still again, he addressed the butler.

"It appears I am entertaining. May I know the names of my guests and the purpose of their visit?"

Ponty, out of countenance for the first time in his life, was at a momentary loss for words. His employer waited, gray eyes unrelenting. After a few seconds the butler spoke.

"Milord, there is a—a situation here at the Manor."

"Indeed?" commented his lordship. "And you cannot handle it?"

Ponty lost color. "A woman has arrived claiming that . . ." He floundered. How do you tell your employer that some strange, common female insists that his lordship's wife is a witch, that she has bewitched half the village as well as his lordship's old nurse, and that the staff is completely disorganized because a gardener's boy has seen a ghost? Ponty, despairing of the task, decided to shift responsibility.

"Milord," he began, "a woman who calls herself Donner has come to—pick up her charge."

"Indeed?" repeated his lordship imperturbably. Ponty felt a surge of envious respect for the cool aristocrat. *Quality! It always shows.* His lordship continued speaking, "Has the woman called Donner informed you of the fact that she is a former servant dismissed in disgrace by me, and currently sought by the London constabulary?"

"No, milord," Ponty confessed humbly. He was beginning to realize the enormity of his blunder in listening to the woman. He could only work now to palliate his offense, and hope for mercy.

But there was more. "Has this disgraced former servant told you the identity of the 'charge' she has gone to such trouble to 'pick up'?"

Ponty grovelled. "Donner's around here somewhere, milord. Perhaps she should tell you herself."

"Ah." His lordship scanned the group of shrinking servants and tenants. "Perhaps she should. Are you there, Donner?"

Boldly the woman thrust herself through the group, spewing veiled threats. "Sure and old Donner was only trying to save your lordship from public shame and misery. I was trying to get *her-we-know-of* safe off to Ireland, in accordance with Your Honor's expressed wish, before worse befell her—and all of us."

Lord John faced her with a look of such contempt that even Donner's thick skin was pierced. Yet the man's voice, when he spoke, was still under rigid control.

"You are all benevolence, ma'am," said Lord John. "However, I fail to see what business you could have here in my house, dismissed from my service as you have been for attempting to practice witchcraft."

Donner's face lit with a smile of triumph. "Well, now, Your Honor dear, since you bring up the subject yourself, 'tis your own good lady's dabbling in witchcraft that I've come to stop. And all these good people with me, to see justice done and the witch confined!"

This was battle with no holds barred. Lord John faced her. "May I remind you that I have the chemist's report on the drug you were giving to Lady Nadine, and witnesses to attest to your attempt to administer the same drug again? I might even remind you that your associate," his eyes flicked scornfully at Adrian, "will be compelled to testify. Perhaps you know how much you may place in his willingness to protect you when his own freedom is at stake."

Donner was quick as an eel. "A fine thing it is, Your Honor, for you to be persecutin' a poor helpless old woman," she began whining.

"Don't waste your time and mine with such nonsense," advised Lord John. "You have made very serious charges in front of these witnesses. The question now is, do you have evidence to back up your charges?"

Donner took them all by surprise. She whirled and pointed to the shadowed area at the top of the stairway. "There she is, the witch, with her dupe, Mag Bennet, about to play their devil's games in front of that accursed portrait! But Donner can control her! Come out, my poor misguided, mad nursling—come to Donner!"

Almost against her will Kathryn advanced into the light. She came down two steps. There was a concerted gasp from the spectators, all of whom had turned their faces up toward the woman on the stairs. In her flaunting finery, white-faced, green-eyed, hair blazing red as flame, she looked more—or less—than human. Lord John, whose eyes had fixed on the beautiful face, maintained his air of stern challenge, but Donner wore a gloating expression of triumph.

"Come to Donner, little changeling!" crooned the old

woman, in a wheedling, loathsome mockery of love, "come, Nadine, I command you!"

But Kathryn was not Nadine, and whatever power the old woman had established over the body and will of her charge was weakened by the mind and spirit of Kathryn. She took one more step down toward the people waiting wide-eyed below. Her own eyes were fastened on the avid face of Donner.

"In the name of all that is good and holy, I charge you to leave this house," Kathryn said clearly, stretching her hand out toward Donner as she had seen Father Percy do. There was a hiss of indrawn breath from those who watched, and a startled light appeared in Lord John's eyes.

"You have no control over my spirit, for it is free and dwells in the light of the God Who gave it life and substance."

"Amen!" Bennet's voice rang out.

Donner, eyes gleaming red in the lamplight, laughed harshly. "Very pretty, little wanton! The Vicar has taught you to mouth the words neatly enough. But your body is soiled, Nadine, and given over to a service more ancient than the Galilean's. Come down, I say!"

Lord John looked from the old crone to the slender girl who stood on the dark stairway. In every inch of his body he ached to help her, but he did not dare to break her concentration. Donner was grinning her wolf-grin. "Answer truly, woman. As your god is your witness, are you indeed Lady Nadine Brionny—or are you *something else?*"

There it was. The one question she must not answer. Kathryn believed firmly that if she told a lie, at this crucial moment, she would increase the power Donner had over Nadine's body. Yet if she told the truth, even Lord John's position and prestige might not be enough to save her from the superstitious fears of the villagers.

The girl stared as if hypnotized into the flat black eyes of the old woman whose lust for power had led her into these dark ways.

And Donner, sure of her victory, smiled. "As your god sees you—and as you hope for heaven—answer! *Are you Nadine Brionny?*"

Into the waiting silence came the sound of a sob. Bennet appeared at the head of the stairs, clasping her Bible to her. Lord John took a step forward, eyes steady on Kathryn's face. The villagers began to whisper and murmur. Kathryn swayed with the intensity of her emotion. Her lips opened.

"I am . . . not . . . Nadine Brionny . . ." she began.

"Then who—or *what*—are you?" Donner's challenge rang out.

The air was heavy with evil. Kathryn lifted her hand to her throat.

"What are you that has seized the body of Lady Nadine?"

There was a growl of animal fear from the crowd. Donner darted to the foot of the stairway.

"Stop!" A strong voice broke the tension. Even Donner turned to face Lord John. He stood smiling confidently up at the white-faced woman on the stairs. "Donner," said the nobleman, "you have asked the wrong questions. There is no longer any Lady Nadine Brionny. There is, however, a Lady Elsingham. I shall ask a few questions—the right ones. *Listen!*"

Never taking his steady eyes from Kathryn's face, he said, "Bennet, I see you have your Bible. Please hand it to milady."

When Kathryn had accepted it into her hands, he addressed her formally. "Madam, swear upon the Holy Book, as God is your witness: are you a Christian soul and no witch?"

Her own eyes holding to his, Kathryn replied in a

voice clearly audible in the breathless silence. "I am a Christian and no witch."

"Are you my true wife—the Lady Elsingham—in spite of all that has happened?" And now the gray eyes were alight with an ardent warmth that brought color to milady's pale cheeks.

—*We have something for each other*—

Kathryn, smiling, answered in a voice whose joy rang like music, "My lord John, as God is my witness, I hope and believe I am." And she took a step toward him, smiling gloriously, and—fell.

"Oh, no!" cried Lord John, between alarm and laughter, *"not again!"*

The villagers, surfeited for once with excitement, and convinced by what they had observed that they had witnessed the healing of a lovers' quarrel, had dispersed to their homes with enough gossip to keep them busy for a twelvemonth. Donner and Adrian Bart, under heavy guard of milord's most trusted menservants, were being driven to London, where they would be given into charge of a magistrate, to be bound over for trial and sentencing. Ponty, reveling in sentiment, had gone to order Cook to prepare an especially tasty late supper for his master and mistress and their guests. At milady's request, the Vicar and Richard Bennet had been sent for, to share the happiness of this hour. Lord John, smiling at his lady with an ardency which brought the roses to her face, said to her, low-voiced, "Supper, yes; guests, of course—I expect Peter and Randall soon—but the moment will come, milady, when you and I must have private converse."

He had carried her to the library and placed her on a comfortable sofa, where she now sat, propped up against cushions, while Bennet hovered solicitously, making sure that none of Kathryn's bones were broken this time. Stretched very much at his ease in a big chair, his eyes still full of that disturbing light, Lord John watched them both. Kathryn found it very hard to meet his elated, masterful gaze.

"Bennet," said Lord John gently, "you have my thanks for your devoted help to Kathryn."

"You believe me now?" interrupted the lady. "You are sure I am Kathryn?"

"I believe," said Lord John. "Your friend Mr. Wilmot Manton has supplied irrefutable proof."

"Bennet believed," said Kathryn, holding out her hand to the beaming woman. "From the beginning. Without proof."

"We will always remember that," answered Lord John with a grateful smile to his old nurse. "As for me, I foresee years of fascinating discussion opening before us, as you teach me what our world will become. But my dear," he warned gently, "I also believe we must keep your true nature a secret, except from our most trusted friends. Eighteenth century London is not ready for a Lady Nostradamus. The average Englishman is hard to convince of the validity of a new idea."

"Yes," agreed Kathryn solemnly, although her eyes shone with laughter, "I *have* noticed that you Englishmen are stubborn and hard to convince. Bull-headed, we call it in the States."

His smile gleamed at her. "Madam, are you declaring war—again?"

Kathryn changed the subject quickly. "And the Vicar believed me. Have you sent for him?"

"Yes," answered her lord. "Perhaps this is he?"

But the commotion at the door heralded the arrival of Lord Peter and Mr. Towne, whom Ponty, again very much master of himself, announced with full decorum.

As soon as the butler had left them, Randall walked over to stand beside the couch on which Kathryn rested. He scanned her face intently. Then he turned to face his host.

"Peter was right," he said. "Johnny, dear boy, I am forced to explode a bombshell. Though this lady is every bit as lovely as your wife, her eyes and expression are completely different from Nadine's. Johnny, I am forced to tell you: this is NOT your wife!"

He could not understand why John, Kathryn and even Bennet broke into hysterical laughter.

While Lord John began to recount the events of the evening, Lord Peter came to Kathryn and kissed her hand. "Welcome home, Kathryn," he said softly. "Can you ever forgive a pair of very arrogant Englishmen?"

"Yes, and love them, too," replied Kathryn, eyes brimming with tears of gratitude at his welcome.

"Better not let our young cockerel hear that," Peter chuckled, and told her Randy's experience with Nadine.

When the Vicar finally arrived, sleepy but full of happiness at the outcome of the situation, the little group sat down to a very gay supper indeed. Only Richard Bennet, late coming, refused to eat and could not keep his eyes off Kathryn. But his quiet smile reassured her that he would never importune her with his love, and she would always have his complete devotion. He left early, pleading urgent duties at the farm. Kathryn watched him leave, his great sturdy body held very straight, and knew a sharp pain in her heart.

The rest of the party behaved with such uproarious good humor that Bennet finally felt compelled to remonstrate. After one particularly outrageous remark by Randy, Bennet said,

"You are all acting like children. You especially, Master Randall. Why can you not behave with as much propriety as Master Peter?"

This sent them off again, but when the laughter quieted, Lord John said lazily, "Yes, why can't you behave, you young whippersnapper? That's my wife you are paying court to."

"Just doing the pretty," grinned Randy.

"Well, go do it to your own girl," Lord John advised him, with such a look of quiet joy on his face that his two friends rejoiced for him.

Lord Peter arose. "Your lady must be tired after all this hubble-bubble. We'll bid you goodnight, now—and offer our best wishes." Standing, he raised his glass. "To the Lady Elsingham, long life and happiness!"

Even Bennet rose with the rest to drink to that.

Finally they were alone, the lovers who had come together across two hundred years. Lord John carried his beautiful wife over the threshold of the great bedroom in which he had been born, and put her down gently on the bed. She could not meet the eagerness in his eyes. He stood looking down at her.

"Kathryn—my beautiful wife—"

She raised her clear lovely eyes to his at last, meeting his ardent gaze. Rich color rose in her cheeks. "We are married—but we are strangers," she said softly.

"Our bodies are not," offered Lord John. "Perhaps we should let them lead us. They have shared joy." It was there in his deepened voice, the urgency of passionate love under iron control. When she did not speak, he sat beside her on the great bed and took her hand gently in his big warm one. "It is like a new wedding night."

The girl nodded, wordless.

He raised her hand to his lips, speaking softly, his breath warm against her palm. Eyes steady on hers, he said, "I, John, take thee, Kathryn, to be my beloved wife—now and for eternity." He released her hand, leaving her free to choose. "And you, my love?"

She looked at this stranger who was her husband, this man with the golden hair and the clear, disturbing gray eyes, the now-familiar mouth sensuous yet disciplined. Her fingers ached to trace the beloved lines and stroke the scarred, lean cheek. Would she take this man?

"Oh, *yes!*" said Kathryn Hendrix of New York, and gave herself into the strength and security of his waiting arms.

Much later, when dawn was shining through the curtains, John said, his lips against the softness of her breast, "You are more beautiful than ever. You are all I have ever hoped for—more than I had dreamed a woman could be..." His voice was curiously soft and roughened. He kissed her gently on the lips, a kiss that sealed his claim upon her. Then his eyes fell on the crumpled orange gown which lay on the floor where he had tossed it the night before. It reminded him of the portrait. He raised himself on one elbow.

"That accursed portrait! How I hated it—and Nadine!—when that jackanapes was painting it! I'll have it destroyed today."

Alarmed, Kathryn sat up beside him. "No! We must be sure to keep it safe, bequeath it in our wills to a museum, with the proviso that it be sent to America in 1975—"

John smiled wickedly. "And why all this bother to

preserve a wretched daub which doesn't do my wife justice?"

"Because, milord," Kathryn smiled demurely, "if we do not, how will I ever get back here into your arms?"

Lord John showed her.